ZEKE PROCTOR:
CHEROKEE OUTLAW

ROBERT J.
CONLEY

POCKET BOOKS

New York   London   Toronto   Sydney   Tokyo   Singapore

This story is based upon actual events. However, some of the characters and incidents portrayed herein are fictitious, and any similarity to the name, character, or history of any person, living or dead, or any actual event is entirely coincidental and unintentional.

An *Original* Publication of POCKET BOOKS

POCKET BOOKS, a division of Simon & Schuster Inc.
1230 Avenue of the Americas, New York, NY 10020

ISBN: 0-671-77901-X

First Pocket Books printing June 1994

10 9 8 7 6 5 4 3 2 1

POCKET BOOKS and colophon are registered trademarks of Simon & Schuster Inc.

Cover art by Tim Tanner

Printed in the U.S.A.

ZEKE PROCTOR:
CHEROKEE OUTLAW

1

Some of them had been gathered there on the front lawn of the capitol long before White Sut Beck made his appearance. They were the early birds from the flock of the curious. Some sat or stood in silence, staring off toward the north end of Tahlequah's main street, the direction from which the two men were expected to arrive, if they showed up at all. And, of course, there was considerable disagreement on that point among those who waited and watched. Some talked in small clusters, speculating on the upcoming events.

"Do you think they'll show up?"

"I don't know. What do you think?"

"They ain't going to show. This crowd here will just hang around and wait till they all get tired out from waiting. Then they'll go on about their own business. That's all."

"Well, if you believe that, then why are you hanging around here?"

1

"I want to see how long everyone else will stick before they realize they've been made out fools."

"Zeke said that he'd be here, and he will. He'll be here. Zeke always keeps his word. I know that. You can say a lot of things about Zeke, but you can't say that he'll tell a lie. You can't say that he'll break his word. I never heard anybody say that about him. Not anyone. Not even a Beck."

"There's going to be a fight here today. I can feel it. Do you think they'll fight?"

"Right here in front of everyone?"

"I don't know. There's been a number killed on both sides. Could be, I guess."

Some of these discussions took place in the English language, some in Cherokee. It was a mixed crowd, this group of the curious and perhaps bored, and it grew steadily as the minutes slowly passed. Soon the main street of the small capital city of the Cherokee Nation was jammed on both sides. An uninformed stranger in town would have thought that a parade was anticipated.

Then, from the far north end of the street, a buggy appeared. Two riders on horseback rode one on each side of the buggy, and two more rode behind. The buggy itself was a two-seater, and it carried two more men. One was the driver. The other, a husky middle-aged man wearing a dark suit, sat beside the driver, his arms crossed over his chest. As the buggy came into closer view, the bystanders could see on the man's face a hard-set, stern expression underneath the small, round-topped, black bowler that sat snugged down on top of his head.

"Here comes one of them," someone shouted.

"Here comes Beck," said another.

A man leaned over close to his nearest neighbor.

"Who's that?" he asked.

"That's White Sut Beck. That's the old man himself."

"Well, where's Proctor?"

"Zeke Proctor ain't showed yet."

"Don't worry. He will."

"Will there be a shoot-out, do you think?"

The buggy stopped in front of the capitol. The four heavily armed riders around it turned this way and that, looking nervously over the crowd for any signs of trouble. One of them rode up close to the bench at the front edge of the capitol square. He looked down at the people sitting on the bench. At last, one of the seated men took the hint and stood up.

"Does Mr. Beck want this bench?" he asked. "We can move off of it if he does."

The rider did not speak, but he gave the man an affirmative nod.

"I'd appreciate it," Beck said from his seat in the buggy.

"Come on," the man at the bench said to his companions. "Let's let Mr. Beck have the bench here. Come on."

The bench was quickly abandoned in deference to White Sut Beck, and two of the riders dismounted, one moving to each end of the bench to stand there stiff like palace guards. The other two riders took the reins of the riderless horses. Beck climbed down out of the buggy with a groan and moved to the bench. The crowd became hushed.

Beck turned toward his driver and nodded. The driver flicked the reins and drove the buggy on down the street. He was followed by the two riders with the

3

four horses. They found a place to park the buggy and tie the horses. Then they walked back to where Beck sat waiting. They walked around behind the bench and turned to face the crowd, which, recognizing the implied threat, moved back. It was almost as if Beck had come to town and set up court.

For a few moments the only noise was the sound of the children running and playing; the tension in the air, felt by the adults, had no effect on them. To children, the much anticipated meeting was of little or no importance. Other things mattered as they moved about in their private world. Somewhere off in the distance a lonesome dog barked. Then one bold man in the crowd spoke out.

"Hey, Beck," he called. "Is Proctor going to show his face in town, do you think?"

One of the armed men behind the bench turned and shot an angry glance in the direction of the offending voice, but before anything else could happen, before anything else could be said, Beck spoke. He did not speak loudly, did not even turn his head. His voice was low and calm, but it was a powerful, resonant voice, and it carried out over the crowd.

"Zeke will be here directly," he said. "Zeke Proctor ain't afraid of no man on earth. He ain't even afraid of the devil."

Then the small groups, which, taken together made up the larger crowd, began again to huddle in close and make their own private conversations in low voices, with hushed tones like the buzzing of so many bees.

"What did he say?"

"Did you hear what he said? What Beck said?"

"He said Zeke's coming."

"He said Zeke ain't afraid of nothing."

"Will they fight?"

"What do you think?"

"I wonder how many men Zeke will bring in with him?"

"If there's a big gunfight, we hadn't ought to be standing around here like this. Someone could get hurt. Someone could get shot with a stray bullet or something."

"Where's the law anyhow? Is the law around?"

"Is that White Sut Beck over there on the bench?"

Then two horses appeared at the north end of town, and once again a hush descended on the crowd. The horses stopped there for a long moment, and even though they made only a dark silhouette at that distance, there was no mistaking the rider, for there was but one rider. The second horse, saddled, was riderless. It was Zeke Proctor all right. Everyone knew.

"There he is," said the armed man standing to the right of Beck.

"I can see," Beck replied.

"He's alone," said the man to Beck's left.

"I can see that too. You all keep your mouths shut."

Then the two horses began to move. They walked down the middle of the street at a slow and leisurely pace. All eyes were on Zeke Proctor as he came closer. He wore tall riding boots and a gray, three-piece suit. On top of his head was a wide-brimmed hat, and around his waist was a gun belt holding two holsters. The holsters contained .45 caliber pearl-handled Colt revolvers, their handles turned toward the front. In his right hand, Zeke carried a Winchester rifle. His dark eyes shifted as he took in the scene around him.

Zeke stopped riding directly across the street from where Beck sat waiting. Sitting in the saddle, he looked Beck right in the face. Then he looked from one to another of the five armed men who stood around his old enemy. He shifted his weight and swung down out of the saddle, keeping his eyes on Beck and his coterie the whole time. Zeke hitched his two horses to the nearby rail, then stood squarely facing Beck.

"I'm not armed, Zeke," Beck said.

Zeke gestured with his rifle toward those around Beck.

"They are," he said.

"They ain't going to do a damned thing," Beck said. "Boys, go wait with the horses."

The five men hesitated, one of them stepping out a little in order to give Beck a look of protestation.

"Go on," Beck said. "You heard me."

The five men looked at one another, shrugged and started walking toward where the horses waited down the street. Zeke Proctor watched them go. When they were about half the distance to their horses, he turned and shoved his Winchester down into the saddle boot on his horse. Then he faced Beck again. Beck stood up and walked out into the street. Halfway across, he stopped.

Zeke looked at Beck. He glanced down the street to where the other men had gone. Then he unbuckled his gun belt. Taking it from around his ample waist, he rebuckled it, turned around and hung it over the saddle horn of his mount. Then he faced Beck again.

Deliberately, Zeke walked out to the middle of the street to meet Beck. He was acutely conscious of all the eyes staring at him and his longtime foe.

He stopped within three feet of the other man and, though it went against the grain of his Cherokee upbringing, stared Beck in the eyes.

"They tell me you got amnesty," Beck said. "A pardon from the president of the United States himself."

"That's what they said over at Fort Smith," Zeke replied.

Beck sighed heavily.

It occurred to Zeke that the last year had aged Beck more than it should have. He looked old and tired. Zeke wondered if it had done as much to him, and if so, was Beck also taking note of it.

"I never thought we'd meet this way," Beck said. "I figured one of us would kill the other sooner or later."

"It sure seemed that way," Zeke replied.

"It goes down hard," Beck said, "but our Cherokee courts acquitted you, and President Grant gave you amnesty."

"That amnesty included you and all your people," Zeke said. "It ain't just directed at me."

"Yeah. Well, I ain't one to go against the government. Not ours and not theirs. It's over, Zeke, and right here in front of all these witnesses, here's my hand on it."

Beck extended his right hand. Zeke looked down at it. He lifted his own right hand and gripped that of Beck. He could hear some gasps from the crowd and then some low muttering. Finally a cheer went up, and everyone gathered there seemed to join in enthusiastically. Zeke thought that Beck's face turned slightly red.

"Well, that's it," Beck said.

Zeke nodded. "Yeah," he said. "It's over."

The two men stood there facing each other for a long, embarrassed moment. Finally Zeke broke the silence.

"Well," he said, "be seeing you."

"Sure," Beck replied. "See you around."

Zeke turned away from Beck and walked back to where he had left his horses. He took his gun belt off the saddle horn and buckled it back on around his waist. Then he climbed up into the saddle, and, taking the reins of the riderless horse, headed out of town, not north, but east.

"You see that?" someone in the crowd said. "I told you. Old Zeke never goes back someplace the same way he come. He always takes a different way back."

"Why's that?"

"He's being careful. That's all. He don't want no one figuring out his movements and laying in wait for him somewhere out on the trail."

Beck looked down the street and waved his arm over his head, and the driver of his buggy climbed into the seat and started the buggy back toward where he stood waiting. The four other men mounted their horses and followed.

As Beck climbed into the buggy, he spoke to his companions.

"It's over with now," he said. "See that everyone knows that. And see that you and all the others remember it. I gave my word. Anyone who makes a move on Zeke Proctor or any of his people will have to answer to me." They rode north out of town.

"That's it?" someone said. "That's all?"

"I don't hardly believe it," another said. "I thought sure there'd be some shooting before it was all over with. I'd have bet money on it."

"Maybe there will be yet. Maybe it ain't over at all."

"It's over all right," said an old man. "They shook hands on it right here in front of all of us, and they both said that it was over. That's all there is to it. It come to an end right here, and we all seen it happen."

As Zeke Proctor rode out of Tahlequah on a lone trail, he too thought, It's over. And he too was convinced of the truth of that simple statement. But he also thought back over the last two or so years. He thought about the things that had happened, and he thought, It's over, but it's been a long, hard time coming.

2

This time, by God, Kesterson had gone too far. Zeke considered himself to be a reasonable man, not quick to anger. He didn't easily fly off the handle, and he had put up plenty with Kesterson's abuses. But there was no getting around it. Kesterson was a no good son of a bitch, a castoff from white society who had moved into the Cherokee Nation looking for someone to live off of without having to do any work for himself.

He had married Zeke's sister Elizabeth, Zeke was sure, just to obtain citizenship rights in the Cherokee Nation. Zeke had known that at the time, and had tried to warn his sister, but Eliza was hard-headed, and she wouldn't listen. She had always been that way.

So she had married James Kesterson, and he had moved in with her on a small farm down in Sequoyah District, almost a hundred miles away from Zeke's home. Zeke hadn't been able to see that much of

10

them, but now and then he visited, and from time to time he heard things. The things that he heard served only to confirm his initial suspicions about the worthless *yoneg,* Kesterson.

But when Zeke did make one of his rare visits to Eliza, she always said that everything was fine. She defended Kesterson, saying that he was doing his best, even though anyone could easily see that the place was run-down and badly neglected.

"Jim's trying real hard," she would say, "but it ain't easy. You know, times is hard, Zeke."

And then there were two children. Zeke worried about his sister and her two little ones. According to old Cherokee ways, Zeke should have been the one to teach them and to discipline them. But there didn't seem to be anything he could do about it. Eliza had made her choice. She had married a white man, and she lived too far away for Zeke to perform his traditional duties or to interfere in any serious way.

Then came the day that Zeke went for a visit, and Kesterson was not there. Eliza had made excuses at first, but finally she had admitted to Zeke that her husband had been gone for some time. He had abandoned her and the children. They were not quite starving, but they were hungry. The place was more run-down than ever, and there was little food in the house. Eliza's clothes and the children's clothes were ragged. Zeke had been furious.

"If I ever see his face again," he had said, "I'll kill him."

Then he had loaded up Eliza and her two children and all of their belongings that were worth loading into a wagon, and he had taken them all back home

11

with him, and that was all right. Everything was all right.

Zeke didn't mind at all taking on the responsibility of the well-being of Eliza and her children. He remembered the old Cherokee clan ways, and he thought that it was only right and proper that he have his sister and his niece and his nephew at home with him where he could properly care for them, at home where they belonged.

And he could easily afford their care. Zeke held and operated three farms in the Goingsnake District of the Cherokee Nation near the Arkansas border, and he managed them successfully and profitably. Under the laws of the Cherokee Nation, there was no private ownership of land, but a citizen could hold as much land as he could make use of, and he could own the improvements to that land.

And no one could say that Zeke was not making proper use of his three farms. The first was the one he had grown up on, his parents' home. It was the home that his mother and father had established after their arrival in the new Cherokee Nation at the end of the Trail of Tears. Zeke had been only seven years old at the time. There he had brought his first wife, Rebecca; and his first daughter, Charlotte, had been born there in 1866.

Then he had married Jane Harlan. Zeke had known the Harlans before the war, and when the war left Jane a widow with two children, he took over her place and turned it into a prosperous farm. There were no laws against multiple marriages in the old Cherokee Nation. It was a time-honored Cherokee tradition for a prosperous, hardworking man to have more than one wife, and Jane needed a husband and father for her children. At this second home, in 1868, Zeke Proctor, Jr., had been born to Jane.

The third farm, Zeke had taken over because it was there to be had, and he was ambitious. And it was to this place that he brought Eliza and her children. In 1872, at the age of forty-one, Zeke Proctor was known widely as a prosperous, progressive, hardworking Cherokee.

And Zeke was well-aware of his reputation. It was not only his sense of tradition and honor that caused him to take on his sister's family. It was his pride as well. He could not have it known around the neighborhood that the sister and the niece and nephew of Zeke Proctor were neglected and living in poverty and shame, that a white man was responsible, and that Zeke had let it all happen. That would never do.

Zeke had the room, the wealth, the ability, and the concern. He could easily support three homes. It made him feel good to do so. It showed all his neighbors that he was a successful and prosperous and honorable man. He was responsible. He took care of his family. Everything was fine.

Fine, that is, until Jim Kesterson dared to show himself again in Zeke's own neighborhood. It was a bold affront, an insult, a challenge to Zeke's pride and honor. It was also at least an implied threat, for who could tell whether or not the man would bother Eliza and the children again? And, of course, it was a thoroughly foolish thing to do, for Zeke had sworn to kill the man, and a threat like that from Zeke Proctor was not a thing to take lightly.

Zeke had learned to handle weapons early in life, and he had taken to them with a natural ease and ability. His father, William Proctor, a white man, had taught him. William had cast his lot with the Cherokees when he had met and married the lovely young Dicey Downing, and when the United States government had forced the Cherokees west over the infamous Trail of Tears, William had gone with them. Zeke, only seven years old, had suffered that cruel removal.

He had watched the aged, the infirm, the very young, sicken and die along the way, but he had endured, and the ordeal had strengthened his body and toughened his spirit.

Then, in their new home in the West, the Cherokees had begun killing each other. The ones who had suffered the forced removal blamed the ones who had signed the fraudulent treaty. They called them the Treaty Party, and after the removal, the newcomers started to kill them. Some called it murder. Others called it assassination. But there was a law in the Cherokee Nation that called for the death of anyone who sold Cherokee land, and those who signed the treaty had sold it all. Because of that, some called the killings executions.

Then, of course, other members of the Treaty Party, their friends and relatives, began to retaliate. They sought to protect themselves. They sought revenge. And so the Cherokee Nation became embroiled in bitter and violent civil strife.

Zeke grew to adolescence during these turbulent and bloody times. They were times that reinforced a young man's natural tendency to want to develop his combative skills, to become a master of violence, to be a warrior.

By the time he was twelve years old—in the wooded

hills of his home, the new Cherokee Nation just west of Arkansas—Zeke could shoot a rifle or pistol better than most men. He could throw a knife or a tomahawk equally well.

Then, just about the time the factional violence in the Cherokee Nation had died down and it was beginning to look like a period of peace, prosperity, and growth for the Cherokees, the Civil War—the War Between the States—broke out in the United States.

John Ross, Principal Chief of the Cherokee Nation, did everything he could to maintain the small nation's neutrality, but Stand Watie, a leader of the old Treaty Party, joined the Confederacy and raised a troop of Cherokee rebels. He was elected Principal Chief of the Confederate Cherokee Nation by his followers, and the Confederate States of America made him a general in their army.

Ross begged the United States government to send troops to protect the neutrality of the Cherokee Nation, and the U.S. was obligated to do so by the terms of the very treaty they had used to justify the Trail of Tears. They did not. And so Union Cherokee troops were raised in opposition to Stand Watie's Confederates.

On July 7, 1862, Zeke Proctor, thirty-one years old, joined Company L, Third Regiment of the Indian Home Guard under the command of Captain Solomon Kaufman. It was an artillery company, and Zeke was enlisted as a private.

At the Battle of Honey Springs, July 17, 1863, Zeke was wounded by a rifle ball in the right shoulder, but the Confederates were defeated there. The victory and the wound and the scar it would leave were things to be proud of. They were the marks of a soldier, of a warrior.

Stand Watie finally surrendered on June 23, 1865, the last Confederate general to do so. The Cherokee Nation had been devastated, practically burned to the ground. Zeke Proctor had been battle-hardened, he had killed, and he had been wounded. And once again, it had been Cherokees fighting Cherokees, Cherokees killing Cherokees.

Zeke was discharged in 1865, and the following year married Rebecca, his daughter Charlotte was born, and he ran for and was elected to the office of sheriff of Goingsnake District of the Cherokee Nation. He served one term, and then returned to farming full-time.

His hair had grown long, well down beyond his shoulders, and he sported a mustache and goatee. He carried two long-barreled, pearl-handled Colt .45 revolvers, their handles toward the front, and he could get them out and put them into play in a hurry. Attached to the band of his broad-brimmed hat were the rattles of four large rattlesnakes, *ujonati,* and everyone around knew that meant big medicine.

Harming a rattlesnake—to a Cherokee, one of the most sacred of animals—was a dangerous taboo. Only certain people among the Cherokees, people with special powers and special knowledge, could kill rattlesnakes. If someone unauthorized dared to do such a thing, or was foolish enough to do it, or did it by accident, terrible harm would befall him.

The presence of the rattles on Zeke's hat, therefore, meant one of two things: either he had the power and the knowledge, or someone else who did was helping

16

to protect him. Either way, the clearly visible rattles gave Zeke a psychological edge over any potential opponent, and added to his already menacing reputation.

And this was the man to whom Jim Kesterson had dared to deliver the supreme insult. Kesterson, the white trash, had first of all presumed to enter the Cherokee Nation, and then to court the sister of Zeke Proctor. Then he had married her. That was enough right there to have caused his death, and Zeke would likely have killed him had it not been for the pleas and the stubbornness of Eliza.

Then Kesterson, after having made two babies with her, abandoned the family. Could the man actually be that stupid? Zeke wondered. Did he not know who it was he was dealing with?

Zeke would have understood had Kesterson left his family and then left the country. But to do what he had done and then to move in practically next door, that was too much.

Somehow, Kesterson had managed to get himself acquainted with Polly Beck. Zeke still thought of her as Polly Beck, even though she had married Steve Hildebrand some years ago. Then Hildebrand had been killed in the war, leaving his widow sole owner of the Hildebrand Mill, a thriving business. And that, of course, was what Kesterson was after.

When Zeke had first heard that Kesterson was living with Polly, he had almost gone after him, but once again Eliza had stopped him.

"Don't do it, Zeke," she had said. "He ain't worth it. Besides that, he is the daddy of my babies. What would it do to them if you was to kill him?"

Zeke grumbled and paced the floor. He had grown

close to his niece and nephew. Eliza was probably right. It wouldn't do for him to kill their father, even if the man was a no-good son of a bitch.

"All right," he had said. "All right. But he'd better keep out of my way. I'm surprised that old White Sut Beck ain't gone over there to kill him anyhow. He ought to think better of his own kin than that."

White Sut was the patriarch of the Beck family. An old mixed-blood family, the Becks followed European family traditions rather than the Cherokee clan system with its matrilineal structure. White Sut was about as wealthy and influential as Zeke was. He was opinionated and stubborn, but no one had ever accused him of dishonesty. During the Civil War, he had fought under Stand Watie on the Confederate side, and because of that he had no use for Zeke Proctor. If the two men passed each other on the street, White Sut would nod curtly and grunt. That was all.

But now Kesterson, who had so wronged the Proctors, had moved in with a Beck woman. So Zeke and White Sut at least had an enemy in common. That was the way Zeke saw it anyway. And the more time went by, the more Zeke wondered why White Sut Beck had not gone to the mill to kill Kesterson. Perhaps, he thought, Polly had prevailed upon White Sut in the same way Eliza had prevailed upon him.

Even so, Zeke thought, if the son of a bitch was living off of my sister right here under my nose, her pleas would do no good. I'd shoot him dead.

Zeke sat in the stage stop at Siloam Springs, Arkansas, a few miles away from his own home. The building itself was actually half in Arkansas, half in the Cherokee Nation. A white stripe down the middle of the floor designated the borderline. Zeke sat on the

Arkansas side of the line. There it was legal to buy and drink whiskey. He sat and he drank.

An Arkansas farmer with whom Zeke was acquainted came into the stage stop.

"Hello there, Zeke," the farmer said.

Zeke looked up. He nodded. He said nothing. He was thinking about Kesterson, and he was surly.

"I just come from the mill," the farmer said. "You know, the one that's run by your brother-in-law."

"Who the hell you talking about?" Zeke said, suddenly belligerent.

"Why, Jim Kesterson, of course. 'Course, I shouldn't say he's running the place. The widow Hildebrand is running it, I reckon. Your brother-in-law's just collecting the money. He sure took mine quick enough."

"Don't call him that again," Zeke said, and the farmer saw then that he was dangerously close to arousing the wrath of Zeke Proctor, the last thing he wanted to do.

"I didn't mean no offense, Zeke," he said. "It's just that I seen him, and I asked him how come he was to move up here so close to where you live, you know, after he went and done your sister the way he done. He just kind of laughed, and then he said, 'Hell, them Indians ain't going to do nothing to me.'"

Zeke left his whiskey on the table. He left the stage stop, mounted up and started riding for the Hildebrand Mill. This time, by God, Kesterson had gone too far.

3

Zeke rode hard for a while, and then he realized that he couldn't afford to run his horse that way. He forced himself to slow his pace even though he was anxious to get to the mill and take care of Kesterson. Eliza was not around to stop him, to make excuses for Kesterson's behavior, to plead with him to think of the children or to tell him that his ruffled feelings were not worth killing a man over. This time, Zeke resolved, nothing would stop him. He would kill the man.

At last he arrived within sight of the mill. He could see two figures out in front of the building. He rode closer, until he could tell that the figures were those of a man and a woman. He kicked his horse in the sides to urge it forward at a faster pace, and when he was close enough to recognize the two people, he pulled back on the reins to halt his mount.

Jim Kesterson, his back toward Zeke, was pointing up toward the top of the mill. Polly Beck Hildebrand was standing not too far away from Kesterson and looking toward where he indicated. Zeke rode in a little closer, stopped again and dismounted.

Kesterson turned toward the sounds behind him and saw Zeke standing there facing him, saw the two guns at Zeke's sides, saw the determination on Zeke's face. He looked down nervously at the handle of his own six-gun stuck in the waistband of his trousers. Then he looked back up, forcing a smile.

"Hello, Zeke," he said.

"I come to kill me a white man," Zeke said.

"Zeke," Polly said, "what's wrong?"

Zeke did not take his eyes off Kesterson as he answered Polly's question.

"You stay out of the way," he said. "You ought to know what's the matter here. Kesterson is married to my sister. He abandoned her and two kids. He's no good, Polly. Get on out of the way."

"I don't know nothing about that, Zeke," she said.

"Hell, Zeke," Kesterson said, "that's old news. Why bring it up again now? Anyhow, me and Liz, we didn't get along too well, you know? It ain't my fault. It ain't hers. Just one of those things."

"You run off and left my sister with two little babies to take care of all by herself," Zeke said. "That's your fault. That's what I'm going to kill you for."

Kesterson began to develop a little more confidence. Zeke was talking. That meant he might not do anything, Kesterson thought. Got to keep him talking.

"Now, Zeke," he said, "if you was going to kill me for leaving Liz, you'd have done it back when I left. You wouldn't have waited till now. Why'd you wait till now, Zeke? Huh?"

"Zeke," Polly said, "we don't want no trouble with you. Why don't you go on home?"

"You get out of the way, Polly," Zeke said. "Go inside. This ain't got nothing to do with you. It's between me and Kesterson. Go on, now."

Polly started walking toward Zeke.

"Zeke," she said, "I've known you all my life."

Kesterson must have thought that Polly's movements distracted Zeke for at least an instant. He grabbed the handle of his revolver, but before he could pull it out, Zeke twisted his right wrist to grip the revolver at his side. He pulled it out in an instant, thumbing back the hammer in the same motion, and leveled it at Kesterson.

"No, Zeke," Polly screamed, jumping toward him, jumping into the path of the bullet just as Zeke squeezed the trigger, taking the full impact of the heavy .45 caliber slug in her chest. She stood stunned for a moment. Her knees weakened and she wobbled on her feet.

"Polly!" Zeke shouted. He stepped forward, putting his arms under her arms, catching her as she collapsed. She fell forward, leaning heavily against his chest, her head limp on his shoulder. "Oh, Polly, I didn't mean to hurt you!"

Kesterson, his eyes wide, stepped backward. Then he turned and ran. Furious at what he, himself, had done, Zeke fired two shots at Kesterson under Polly's arm. Kesterson kept running. He ran into the mill, slamming the door shut behind him. Zeke thought for a moment about chasing the man, then his attention returned to the woman he held in his arms.

Carefully, gently, he laid Polly down on the ground.

She did not move. He looked into her eyes, but they were glazed.

"Polly," he said. There was no response. He leaned his face close over hers to listen or to feel for a breath. There was none. Polly Beck Hildebrand was dead.

Jack Wright, sheriff of Goïngsnake District, was returning home. He had gone to check a fence for legal height after having received a complaint from a farmer that his neighbor's hogs were getting into his garden. He was tired, and he was wondering whether or not his meager salary was worth all the headaches that came with the job. He had climbed off his horse and was about to lead it out to the barn when he heard the sound of hooves behind him. He looked over his shoulder and saw Zeke Proctor riding down his lane.

"Zeke," he said as the rider drew near, "what brings you around?"

"I come to turn myself in, Jack," Zeke said. He reined in his mount and swung down out of the saddle. "I just killed Polly Beck."

Jack Wright knew Zeke Proctor. He knew him as a former lawman and as an honest, hardworking farmer. He also knew that Zeke had a well-deserved reputation as a skilled man of arms. He was astonished at the confession he heard from Zeke, though.

"Polly Beck?" he said. "Hildebrand?"

"Yeah," Zeke said. "You want my guns?"

"No. No," Wright said. "Come on inside out of the cold. We'll have a cup of coffee, and you can tell me all about it."

They put the two horses in the barn and went inside. Mrs. Wright already had coffee made, so

Wright and Zeke sat at the table facing each other. Mrs. Wright gave them each a cup of coffee.

"Thanks," Zeke said.

"You said you killed her," Wright said. "Why?"

"I didn't mean to kill Polly," Zeke replied. "I was aiming for Jim Kesterson. She jumped in the way."

"Where did this happen?"

"At the mill."

"Where's Kesterson?"

"He run off. He ran into the mill, but then he ran out the back way. I don't know where he's at now."

"You sure Polly's dead?" the sheriff asked.

"She's sure dead," Zeke replied.

"What'd you do with her? With the body, I mean?"

"I left her laying there, but before I come here, I sent word to her people. They'll be taking care of her."

"Damn it," Wright said. "I knew there'd be trouble when that Kesterson moved in out there."

"He's no good," Zeke said. "I wish she hadn't got in the way. I'd have killed him for sure. I'll still kill him if I ever get another chance."

"All right," the sheriff said. He took a final sip of his coffee and stood up. "You go on home. I'll send a couple of men out to guard your house. Not that I think you'll try to run off."

"I know," Zeke said. "It's procedures."

"Yeah. I'll let you know when we get a trial date set. In the meantime, go on about your business. Just don't give my guards the slip. They'll be following you everywhere you go."

"Yes," Zeke said. "I know. I'll treat them like they was my guests."

Zeke rode home. Shortly after he arrived there, two riders came up. They were heavily armed. Zeke

24

stepped out the front door of his house and waved a greeting.

"Come on in, boys," he said. "Supper's almost ready."

White Sut Beck shoved a shell into his shotgun. His younger brother Bill was strapping a gun belt around his waist. Aaron Beck, old, white-haired, and crippled with arthritis, sat in a chair in the corner of the room.

"Where is Zeke?" Aaron asked.

"What?" White Sut said, shoving another shell into the shotgun and snapping the gun shut.

"I said, where is Zeke at now?"

"I don't know," White Sut replied, "but I'll find him if he's this side of hell."

"I reckon he's gone home," Bill said. "They said he turned himself in to Jack Wright, and then Wright sent him on home. He sent two guards after him."

"Then Zeke's under arrest," Aaron said, "and there's going to be a trial."

"He'll be a dead man before they can get a date set," White Sut said. "Come on, Bill." He headed for the door.

"Sut," Aaron said, his voice sharp and commanding, "put them guns away."

White Sut Beck paused, hesitant to ignore the old man's order. Bill stood to one side waiting to see what his brother would do.

"You hear me?" Aaron said. "Zeke turned himself in. He's under arrest, and there's going to be a trial. That's the way it ought to be."

"He killed Polly," Sut said. "The way it ought to be is I ought to kill him."

"No, Sut. We got laws, and we Becks is going to live by the law. Now do as I say."

Sut made a disgusted sound, but he turned around and walked back to the gun rack. He hesitated a moment, then hung up the shotgun. "All right," he said. "I'll wait for the trial, but if the law don't hang him, I will kill him."

Sut opened a bureau drawer and took out a pipe, tobacco pouch, and a few wooden matches. He headed for the door again.

"Where you going now?" Aaron asked.

"I'm going to set on the porch and smoke."

Sut had nearly finished his pipe when his nephew Sam came peeking around the corner of the house.

"Uncle Sut?"

Sut looked over his shoulder. "Sam," he said. "What are you doing there?"

"Lookie here who I got, Uncle Sut." Sam turned to look behind him, around the corner of the house, and he spoke to someone there. "Come on," he said. "Come on out. It's okay."

Jim Kesterson stepped out from behind the corner and walked around to stand beside Sam, in front of White Sut Beck. Sut frowned. He had never liked Kesterson. Like Zeke Proctor, Sut thought that Kesterson was trash, a white man who tried to live off Cherokee women. He had known about Kesterson's marriage to Eliza Proctor and his desertion of his wife and two children. He had not liked it when the man had moved in with Polly. But things were different now.

"Kesterson," he said, "what are you doing here?"

"I need protection," Kesterson said. "Zeke Proctor's killed Polly, and he'll kill me if he can."

"He was trying to kill you, wasn't he?"

"Well, yeah, I guess. He just started shooting."

"And you run off. Why didn't you stop him?"

"I ain't no match for Zeke," Kesterson whined. "You know that."

"Soon as you moved in with Polly," Sut said, "I should have killed you myself. It's too late now."

"Uncle Sut," Sam said, "Jim can go with us when we go after old Zeke. It'd be one more gun."

"We ain't going," Sut said. "Aaron says we have to wait for the trial. Let the law hang Zeke."

"What if they don't?" Sam asked. "Zeke's got a lot of friends. He used to be the sheriff."

"Hell, I know that," Sut said. "Aaron says wait, and we're going to wait. If the law don't hang Zeke, then we'll go after him. That's the last word on it."

"There's another way," Kesterson said.

Sut stood up and stepped down off the porch. He walked up close to Kesterson and looked him hard in the eyes. Kesterson ducked his head and shuffled his feet nervously.

"What are you talking about?" Sut asked.

"I ain't a Cherokee," Kesterson said. "I'm a white man."

Sut sneered. "We know what you are," he said. "You're a *yoneg.*"

"We can swear out a complaint against Zeke in the federal court over at Fort Smith," Kesterson said.

"Zeke killed Polly," Sut said, "and Polly's a Cherokee. The Cherokee courts have jurisdiction over that."

"Yeah," Kesterson replied, "I know that. But he was trying to kill me. That's attempted murder. The charge against Zeke in Fort Smith would be attempted murder on a white man. You see?"

"What do you think, Uncle Sut?" Sam asked.

Sut turned and walked away from Kesterson. "If Jim wants to file charges over in Fort Smith," he said, "that's his business."

"I'm scared to go by myself," Kesterson said. "I need protection."

"Well?" Sam said.

"All right," Sut replied. "First thing in the morning, we'll ride to Fort Smith. All of us."

4

Zeke Proctor sat on his front porch in an old straight-backed wooden chair with a woven cane seat. He was smoking a corncob pipe. The two guards sent out by Sheriff Wright lounged, one on each end of the porch. The guard to Zeke's right was drinking a cup of coffee. The scene was relaxed, not at all tense. The sky to the east had a reddish hue just above the tree line, where the sun was rising to start the day. There was a slight chill in the morning air.

"Seems like it's going to warm up a little today," said the guard with the coffee.

"Seems like," Zeke said, "but it'll get cold again before the summer comes on us, I guess."

He puffed on his pipe and watched the smoke rise. Pretty soon the fire in the pipe bowl went out. Zeke leaned over, reaching down to tap his pipe lightly on the edge of the porch, loosening and then knocking out the burnt tobacco. Then he stood up and tucked the warm pipe into a pocket.

"I'll go inside and see how Rebecca's doing with our breakfast," he said. He opened the door and went into the house. In another minute he opened it again and stuck his head out. "Come on in, boys," he said. "It's on the table. Eggs and sausage, biscuits and gravy, grits and 'taters. And lots of coffee. Come on in and sit down."

They all sat down around the table together to eat: Zeke, six-year-old Charlotte, two-year-old Francis, and the two guards, Cull and Frog. Rebecca did not sit down. She was busy serving the meal and tending to the wants and needs of the triplets, Linnie, Minnie, and Willie, only about two months old. She had her hands full.

They ate their fill and drank plenty of coffee. Then they talked.

"I've got a load of wool ready to go to the mill at Shilo," Zeke said. "You boys going to ride along with me over there?"

"Sure, Zeke," Cull replied.

"Sheriff didn't tell us to keep you here," Frog said, "only that we was to stay with you."

"Zeke," Rebecca said, a baby in each arm, "I don't think you should go across the line. I heard that Jim Kesterson was going to the federal court to swear out a warrant for you."

Charlotte was holding the third baby, and she carried her out onto the porch.

"I'm already under arrest here," Zeke said. "They can't arrest me over there for the same thing, can they?"

"Well," Cull said, "I ain't too sure, but I think that maybe they can."

"If they want to," Frog said, "they will, if they get a chance."

"If Kesterson has really sworn it out," Cull said. "Do you know if he's done that?"

"I don't know for sure," Rebecca replied, "but I heard that he was going to. Besides that, I wouldn't be surprised if some of them Becks was out there waiting to catch Zeke on the road somewhere."

"Well," Frog said, "I sure wouldn't put that past old White Sut Beck."

"White Sut won't do anything like that," Zeke said. "He'll wait and see how the trial comes out. Aaron won't let him do it any other way. And anyhow, I can take care of myself."

"Just the same," Rebecca said, "I think I'll take the wagon over there to Shilo. I can drive it all right. It's loaded already, and they'll do the rest for me on over at the mill."

"I don't know," Zeke said.

"It's the best way," she said. "I'll get Jodie to ride along with me."

"Jodie?" Cull said. "Your little brother?"

"He's fourteen now," Rebecca said. "He's a good helper, and good company too. We'll manage everything all right."

Zeke scratched the short beard on his chin and looked thoughtful.

"Well, all right," he said. "I guess I don't need any more trouble than what I got already."

"That's for sure," Cull said. "Say, Rebecca, can I have another cup of that coffee?"

White Sut Beck, Bill Beck, Sam Beck, and Jim Kesterson tied their horses at the hitch rail in front of the red-brick federal courthouse in Fort Smith, Arkansas. White Sut walked to the foot of the stairway that led up to the massive front doors, hitched up his trousers, then mounted the steps. The others followed.

Inside, White Sut walked through the open door of the first office he came to. The man sitting behind the big desk looked up.

"Can I help you?" he said.

"Where do we go to file charges on someone?" White Sut asked.

"They'll have to be filed with Mr. Churchill, the U.S. Commissioner," the man said, "but I can start the paperwork for you right here."

"Then let's get to it," White Sut said. He turned slightly, reaching back to take Kesterson by the shoulder, and then he hauled Kesterson up in front and shoved him toward the desk. "Tell him," he said.

The man behind the desk looked questioningly at Kesterson.

"Well," Kesterson said, "it was Zeke Proctor."

"That's who the complaint is against?" the clerk asked.

"Ezekiel Proctor," White Sut said, "a citizen of the Cherokee Nation."

The clerk wrote in a slow and tedious hand. Then he looked up again.

"Which one of you gentlemen is making the complaint?" he asked.

Kesterson looked nervously at White Sut.

"He is," White Sut said, jabbing a thumb into the air in the direction of Kesterson. The clerk cocked his head and looked at Kesterson, waiting. When Kesterson said nothing, the clerk spoke again.

"Do you have a name?"

"Yeah," Kesterson said. "Sure I do. Uh, it's Kesterson. Jim Kesterson."

"Is it James?"

"Oh. Yeah."

"Spell it, please. Not James, but Kesterson."

Kesterson did, and the clerk wrote for a while. Then he looked up again.

"And what exactly is the nature of the complaint?" he asked.

"Uh, what?" Kesterson said.

"Tell him what Zeke did," White Sut said.

"Oh, yeah," Kesterson said. "Well, he shot at me. He tried to kill me. He took three shots at me. The first one I was facing him. The next two he shot at my back. He sure enough tried to kill me."

"Did any of the three shots actually strike you?" the clerk asked.

"Well, no, but he tried. It ain't because he didn't try. He hit my woman with his first shot and killed her. Killed her dead right there in front of me. He was aiming at me. But she's a Indian, so they arrested him over there in the Cherokee Nation on a murder charge for killing a Indian woman. But I'm a white man, and he tried to kill me, and he ought to be charged with that too. That was what his real intention was in the first place."

"Assault with intent to kill," the clerk said as he wrote. He asked some more questions, mostly about the time and place of the incident, and then he wrote for, what seemed to White Sut Beck, a painfully long time. Then he turned the paper around and had Kesterson sign his name to it. That done, he took up the document and stood up.

"Wait here for a moment, please," the official said, and he left the office.

"Where the hell's he going with that?" Kesterson asked.

"Never mind," White Sut said. "Just shut up and wait."

In a short while the clerk returned. He no longer had the document in his hand.

"Follow me, please," he said. "The commissioner would like to speak with you."

He led them down the hall and around a corner to another office. He opened the door and stepped inside, motioning the Becks and Kesterson to step in.

"Mr. Churchill," he said, "this is Mr. James Kesterson. These gentlemen came with him. Your names?"

"I'm White Sut Beck. This is my brother Bill. My nephew Sam."

"All right, Oliver," Churchill said, nodding. Oliver the clerk, with a toss of his head, went out of the office and shut the door behind him. Churchill glanced at the paper on his desk. Then he looked up at Kesterson, and from Kesterson to each of the Becks.

"I'm James Churchill," he said, "United States Commissioner for the Western District of Arkansas. Mr. Kesterson, would you describe to me exactly what happened when Mr. Proctor made this attempt on your life?"

"Well, sir," Kesterson said, shooting a quick and furtive glance at White Sut Beck, "I was out in front of the mill with my—with the woman who owns the mill: Polly, the widow Hildebrand."

White Sut Beck clenched his teeth, tightening his

jaws, but Kesterson failed to see the hard expression on his face. He went on.

"We was looking up at the roof and talking about some work that needed to be done up there. Just minding our own business. Not bothering no one. Hell, we was at home. Our own home. Well, Zeke come riding up."

"Was he alone?" the commissioner asked.

"Yes, sir, he was," Kesterson replied. "He was all by himself, but he was wearing them two guns the way he does, with the handles poking out toward the front, you know. And he come right up to where we was standing out there in the yard, and he got off his horse. Right away he commenced to arguing with me. He said he come to kill me."

"Did he say why he wanted to kill you?" the commissioner asked.

"Well, no. Not exactly. No, sir. But he's had it in for me for some time now. I think he didn't want me living so close to him. That's what I think. You know, he's Indian, and he don't like white folks. He said, 'I'm going to kill me a white man.' That's what he said when he first rode up. 'I'm going to kill me a white man,' he said."

Churchill was taking notes while Kesterson talked. He was not so meticulous as Oliver had been, and so he was not so slow.

"Go on," he said.

"Well, I tried to talk to him, but he wouldn't listen. You know, I tried to talk him out of fighting. I didn't want to fight with him. He's a bad killer. He's killed a bunch of people before he come after me and killed Polly. Directly, he pulled out a pistol and shot at me,

35

but he missed. He hit Polly instead. I took off running, and he shot twice more at me, but I got away. That's about it."

"Mr. Proctor is a citizen of the Cherokee Nation," Churchill said, "and you are not. Is that correct?"

"That's right," Kesterson replied. "I'm a white man. Pure white."

"Are you a U.S. citizen, Mr. Kesterson?"

"Why, hell yes, I am."

"And Mrs. Hildebrand was a Cherokee citizen?"

"Yes. Yes, she was. Yes, sir."

"And Mr. Proctor has been arrested by Cherokee authorities?"

"Yeah."

"For the murder of Mrs. Hildebrand?"

"That's right."

"But not for assault on you?"

"No, sir. Not for that. They told me that the Cherokee courts can't arrest him for that because I'm white."

"That's correct, Mr. Kesterson. And now you want me to issue a warrant for his arrest for assault with intent to kill?"

"Yes, sir. I guess that's what you call it. Salt."

Churchill turned his head toward White Sut Beck. "Mr. Beck, was it?"

"That's right," White Sut replied.

"May I ask what your interest is in this case?"

"Mrs. Hildebrand was Polly Beck," White Sut said. "She was a close and dear relative of mine. My interest is to see that justice is done. Zeke Proctor is a wealthy and influential man. He was once the sheriff of Goingsnake District himself. He has friends in high places in the Cherokee Nation and especially in the

Goingsnake District. After the shooting, he calmly turned himself in to Jack Wright, the current sheriff of Goingsnake District. The two men are old friends, good friends. Technically, he's under arrest, but he's actually at home with two guards who are also his friends, waiting for a trial date. I'm afraid that when he's tried in our courts, he'll be acquitted."

"I see," Churchill said. He rubbed his chin, staring at the paperwork in front of him.

"Mr. Kesterson, Mr. Beck," he said, "I'm going to issue a warrant for the arrest of Ezekiel Proctor on the charge of assault with intent to kill against the person of a white man and not a citizen of the Cherokee Nation. I'm going to give this warrant to Marshal Roots with instructions to send two deputies into the Cherokee Nation to observe the trial of Ezekiel Proctor in the Cherokee courts. They will not attempt to serve the warrant unless the outcome of the trial is favorable to Ezekiel Proctor. Should he be acquitted of the murder charge in the Cherokee courts, then the deputies will serve the warrant on him. They will arrest him on this federal charge of assault.

"Mr. Beck, justice will be done. If Ezekiel Proctor is guilty of these charges, one way or another, he will pay. The federal court is determined to bring law and order to the Indian Territory."

5

Rebecca Proctor could handle a team of mules about as well as any man, but Jodie was bored with the ride and had begged her to let him drive. And so she did. She watched him as he took the reins. He was at a difficult age, she knew, but he was a good boy, and it did him good, she was sure, to take on responsibilities. It made him feel like a man, and that feeling, in turn, made him act a little more mature and sensible.

"Well, how am I doing?" Jodie asked, a wide, proud grin on his face.

"You're doing fine," Rebecca said. "A little more practice and you'll be right up there with the best of them."

"Can I drive right on into town and up to the mill?"

"Not tonight," Rebecca said. "We won't be going to the mill tonight. It'll be closed up before we can get there."

"I know that. I mean in the morning. Can I drive it in come morning?"

"Sure you can," Rebecca replied. "Why not?"

"You know, sis, I'm really glad you asked me to come along with you on this trip."

"Me too," Rebecca said. "You're a big help to me. I didn't want Zeke coming into Arkansas, so that meant that I had to·do it instead. And I could do it myself, but I'm sure relieved to have your help, though. And your company."

Jodie gave a flick of the reins.

"Glad to do it, sis," he said.

Shilo was just ahead. It was already late in the evening. Rebecca knew, as she had told her brother earlier, that the mill would be closed for the day. She also knew that a good campsite was there to be had at the edge of town beside a pleasant creek. She liked the spot, and had used it before with Zeke.

She had Jodie pull the wagon off the road and gather wood for a small campfire. They would spend the night there and drive into town to the mill first thing in the morning. Everything was going well. There had been no problems. Of course, she had not expected any.

They made their camp and ate a frugal meal. Jodie was still hungry, and so Rebecca was planning to prepare more for him. Then suddenly she doubled over with an intense pain in her left side. It was so sharp and unexpected that she cried out before she could stop herself. Jodie ran to her, offering his support, his face showing his fear.

"What is it, sis? What's wrong?"

It took her a moment to answer. She took a few deep breaths, and slowly she tried to straighten up and smile. The smile was feeble at best.

"Oh, it's nothing, I'm sure," she said. "I'm okay now. I just had a pain in my side, that's all. Don't worry, Jodie. I'm fine."

"Are you sure?"

"Of course I'm sure. Now sit back down and let me fix you a little more supper. You're still a growing boy. I should have fixed you more to start with. I don't know what I was thinking about. It won't take long, though."

She walked back to the wagon for more supplies, and on the way she felt a couple more pangs. She tried to hide them from her brother, but he could tell. He opened his mouth as if to speak, but he could think of nothing to say.

Then it hit her again. Her knees grew weak and she grabbed onto the side of the wagon to keep from falling. She groaned out loud. She couldn't help herself. The pain was too intense. Again Jodie ran to her.

"Sis?" he said.

"Get me up in the wagon, Jodie," she said, talking between gasps for breath.

He helped her climb up onto the seat, and she doubled over, her head almost between her knees.

"What do I do?" Jodie asked, his voice betraying near panic.

"Drive," she said. "Take me to the Harrises. Hurry."

Jodie knew the Harrises. He knew where they lived in Shilo. They were friends of the Proctors, and Jodie had met them before on trips into Shilo with his sister and her husband. He lashed at the mules frantically with the reins and shouted at them to get a move on.

He drove them as fast as he dared, and when he reached the house, he jumped down from the wagon seat, raced around to help his sister down, and shouted out all at the same time.

"Mr. Harris! Mr. Harris! Hurry up! Please."

Walt Harris came out of the house, followed by his wife. "Jodie?" he said. "That you? What's the matter here?"

"It's Rebecca. She's sick."

They took her into the house and put her in a bed, and Walt Harris rushed out for the nearest doctor. But it was too late. Sometime in the middle of the night, Rebecca Proctor died.

"Cramp cholera," the doctor said. "It comes on them sudden like that. Not much can be done about it, I'm afraid. Sorry."

"What am I going to do?" Jodie asked, tears running down his face.

"Take my saddle horse," Harris said, "and ride back to tell Zeke. He has to know. I'll take care of things here until someone comes back."

Zeke Proctor was awakened in the early morning hours by the sound of pounding hoofs, and he and both guards were outside with guns in their hands when Jodie rode up to the porch calling Zeke's name. They recognized the boy and lowered their guns. Jodie practically fell out of the saddle into Zeke's arms.

"What's happened, boy?" Zeke asked. "Where's Rebecca?"

"She's dead, Zeke," Jodie said. He was still sobbing. "She's dead."

"Dead?" Zeke said. "Rebecca?"

"In Shilo at the Harrises. The doc said cramp cholera."

"I got to go get her," Zeke said.

"No," Jodie said. "She didn't want you going over there. I'll go on home and get Pa and my brother. We'll go get her."

"That's best," Cull said.

"You can't do no more than they can," Frog added.

Zeke paced a moment, looking distracted. Then he put a hand on Jodie's shoulder.

"Go on then, boy," he said, and, as if in a daze, he turned and walked toward the side of the house to stand alone in the darkness as his burning eyes filled with tears.

"Zeke?" Cull said.

"Leave him alone," Frog said.

Once again, young Jodie disappeared in the darkness, riding toward home to carry his sad message to the rest of his family.

White Sut Beck was in Tahlequah. Bill and Sam had gone in with him, and they tied their horses to the hitch rail on Muskogee Avenue across from the capitol building.

"You two stay here," White Sut said. "I'll take care of this."

He crossed the street alone and walked across the square to reach the front door of the two-story brick building. Inside, he walked to the chief's office and stepped boldly inside.

Lewis Downing, Principal Chief of the Cherokee Nation, looked up from his work.

"Oh, hello, Sut," he said. "What brings you down this way?"

"It ain't a social call," Sut replied. "You know about Zeke Proctor's trial coming up?"

"Yes, I do," Downing said. "It's a bad business. I was sorry to hear about Polly, Sut."

"Yeah. Thanks. Who's slated as judge for the trial? Has that been decided? Do you know?"

Chief Downing shuffled some papers on his desk, but he didn't appear to really consult them before he answered Beck's question.

"Yes," he said. "I believe it's Jim Walker. He's a good man. A good judge."

"Maybe so, but he's related to Zeke Proctor," Beck replied. "I want him replaced."

"That's not going to be easy to do, Sut," the chief said. "Besides, I don't think you have to worry about Jim. He won't let anything like that interfere with his decisions. I know him real well. He's—"

"If he ain't replaced before the trial," White Sut said, interrupting the chief, "I'll lodge a protest on the basis of his relation to Zeke Proctor. And if Jim Walker's the judge and Zeke gets off, I'll do more than that. And this ain't no idle threat, Lewis. You know I mean what I say."

"All right. All right," Downing said. He heaved a heavy sigh. "I'll see what I can do. I'll have to call a special council meeting to discuss the case and get another judge appointed. You know that, don't you? It'll take some time. We might even have to postpone the trial date."

"We got time," White Sut said. "More time than patience. I'd have gone after Zeke myself already except for Aaron. Aaron said we wait for the trial, so we'll wait. But by God, it had better be a fair one, so take all the time you need to make it fair."

"It will be, Sut," Downing said. "Fair to both sides. You have my word on that."

In Fort Smith, Arkansas, Deputies Jacob G. Owens and Joseph Peavy reported to United States Marshal Logan Roots in his office at the federal courthouse. They stood in front of his big desk, their hats in their hands. Roots continued writing for a moment after they had entered. Finally he put down his pen and looked up.

"Sit down, boys," he said.

Awkwardly, the two deputies dragged chairs up to the desk and sat. There was another moment of nervous silence.

"Uh, you sent for us, Marshal Roots?" Peavy asked.

"Yes," Roots said, "I did. I've got a job for you two men. It's a touchy one. That's why I sent for you two."

"What is it?" Owens asked.

"You heard about the killing at the Hildebrand Mill over in the Cherokee Nation?"

The two deputies looked at one another. Then Peavy spoke.

"Yeah," he said. "Ol' Zeke Proctor shot a Cherokee woman—Polly Hildebrand. That's what I heard."

"That's right," the marshal said.

"Well, what's that got to do with us?" Owens asked. "Two Indians. That's a case for the Cherokee courts, ain't it?"

"Yes," Roots replied. "It is. But Zeke Proctor never meant to kill the Hildebrand woman. He was shooting at a white man named Jim Kesterson. The woman got in the way. At least, that's the way Kesterson tells it. He swore out a warrant for the arrest of Proctor on the charge of assault with intent to kill a white man."

44

"And you want us to serve it on him?" Peavy asked.

"I want you to carry it with you," Roots said. "Don't say a word about it to anyone. Go over there and watch. See what happens at the trial. If the Cherokees find Proctor guilty of murder and hang him for it, then you tear up that warrant and forget about it. But if he gets off of that murder charge, you slap him with that federal warrant right away. You understand me?"

"Yes, sir," Owens said. "We hide and watch until the Cherokee courts are done with their case. If they find him guilty, we don't do a damn thing."

"Except come right back here and tell me what's happened," Roots said.

"Sure," Owens replied. "But if they should let him off, then we arrest him on this here warrant and bring him on in. Right?"

"That's it."

"When do we leave, Marshal?" Peavy asked.

"First thing in the morning," the marshal replied. "You got time to get yourselves ready yet this evening?"

"Plenty of time," Owens said.

"We'll be on our way before the sun's up," Peavy said.

"All right," Roots said. "Be careful, then, and good luck to you."

Owens tucked the warrant into an inside coat pocket, and he and Peavy stood up almost together. They each gave the marshal a polite and slightly awkward nod, then turned and walked out of the office. In the hallway, they put their hats back on their heads. Peavy reached into his pocket for a plug of tobacco. He bit off a chew.

45

"Jake," he said, "you know old Zeke Proctor?"

"Not personal," Owens replied, "but I've heard of him aplenty. They say he's a tough one."

"Well, I know him," Peavy said, softening up his chaw in his mouth, "and whatever wild tales you heard about old Zeke, he's a damn site tougher than that. This ain't going to be no picnic old Logan has sent us on."

"I didn't expect he was doing us a favor," Owens said.

The two men walked outside, and Peavy spat out a dark stream on the grass.

"Better bring along your camping gear," he said. "This business could take us a little while."

"Yeah," Owens said. "Camping gear and plenty of guns and shells. Just in case. What time you want to head out in the morning?"

"Oh, five sound all right?"

"It's all right with me. Meet you at the stable?"

"Yeah," Peavy said. He spat again. "The stables at about five. See you there, pardner."

Jake Owens stood for a moment watching Joe Peavy amble away. Maybe, he thought, all of their elaborate preparations would be for nothing. Maybe the Cherokee courts would find Zeke Proctor guilty of murder and hang him for it. Maybe, in spite of what Joe Peavy said and in spite of Logan Roots's precautions, this would turn out to be a picnic after all. A kind of a vacation. Maybe.

6

From his father, William Proctor, Zeke had learned the way the white man reasons, and he knew that according to that system of belief, Rebecca would have been stricken with the killing cramp cholera even had she not made the wagon trip to the mill at Shilo. She would have died at home. And her death, coming when it did, was an unfortunate coincidence. It had nothing to do with the killing of Polly Beck or anything else. That was the way of things according to the white man's reasoning process.

But Zeke had followed his mother in his beliefs, and he could not make himself think like a white man. He could tell himself how a white man would think, how a white man would explain things, but he still couldn't accept it; couldn't believe it himself. And to Zeke's mind, to the Cherokee mind, there was no such thing as coincidence. Everything that happened, happened for a specific reason. There was a single, definite cause for every single effect.

Furthermore, wrong behavior by an individual, whether purposeful or simply careless, could cause bad things to happen to anyone and everyone around him. Each individual was, therefore, in a very real sense, responsible for the well-being of his entire community, for the health of the entire world, for that matter. Certain things must be done. Certain things must not be done. Everything had to be kept in proper balance. An eye for an eye. A tooth for a tooth. A life for a life. Zeke Proctor had killed Polly Beck, and even though he had not meant to kill her, he had done it. He was responsible.

And then Rebecca had died, stricken down unexpectedly, suddenly and mysteriously. A life for a life. Could it be? Perhaps. Perhaps that was the way in which Zeke had been forced to pay for the life of Polly Beck. The white man's doctor had called it cramp cholera, and he had said that it happens like that. It was a casual and easy explanation.

But Zeke could not bring himself to accept that explanation. He saw a definite and specific and palpable relationship between the sequential events, and, as a result, he felt responsible for the death of his Rebecca as well as for that of poor Polly Beck. At the very least, he thought, he should not have allowed Rebecca to drive to Shilo without him.

Of course, he also believed that if something was meant to happen, it would happen, no matter what he or anyone else tried to do to prevent it. Human efforts were no match for the mysterious powers of the universe. And in a way, that was a comforting thought. And there was the belief that each individual was born with an allotted number of years to live. If that was true, as Zeke had heard, then Rebecca's time simply had come, or else, if her time had been cut short, she would be born again in order to fill out her remaining years.

So where was the truth? He did not know. Some of the things that he had previously thought that he believed now seemed to contradict each other. Still, he felt responsible and more than a little guilty.

Then there was Jim Kesterson. Certainly, Zeke thought, Kesterson had to share in the blame. Or perhaps, Zeke thought, his real fault was that he had failed to eliminate Kesterson in the first place, way back when the white man had first courted his sister. There were sins of omission as well as commission.

But if all things happened as they were meant to happen, and he had killed Kesterson way back then when the thought had first occurred to him, Elizabeth's two children would never have been born, and no matter who their father was or what he was like or what he had done and failed to do, they were fine children, and Zeke loved them.

But he missed Rebecca. He missed her terribly. It was not just that she had been a good wife and a good mother. It was not just that he would have to take on more responsibilities around the house without her there. She had been a joy and a comfort. He would miss her, he knew, for a good long time.

Rebecca's people had gone to Shilo and returned with her body. They had laid it out in Zeke's house, and for four days and nights Zeke and other members of the family had sat up with her. Her soul, it was said, would return on the fourth day for a last visit before its final departure to the world of the spirits. It should not return to an empty house or a sad house.

* * *

They had gone to the ceremonial ground nearby, where the sacred fire burned in the center. Around the ground were seven arbors, one for each of the seven clans. The body, in a casket, was carried in from the west, the seven pallbearers walking with it toward the fire. Nearing the fire, they turned south in order to circle the fire in a counterclockwise motion. They stopped on the east, placing the casket on a bier of stacked logs that had been prepared there for the occasion. The head was toward the fire. The feet pointed east.

Between the casket and the fire four men stood in line. First, to the south, was the headman of the ceremonial ground. To his right stood a translator, for not everyone gathered there would be able to understand the Cherokee language. Next was the community chief, and finally, northernmost, stood the medicine man, who was also the keeper of the fire.

The seven pallbearers, one from each of the seven clans, stood lined up on the north side of the casket. All of these men, and all of the men in the crowd of mourners gathered there, wore hats. Then the headman removed his hat, and so did all of the other men present. The headman was about to speak.

He spoke in the Cherokee language, and the things he said were based partly on ancient Cherokee beliefs and partly on the teachings of the Christian missionaries. He spoke words of praise for Rebecca Proctor. She was a good, hardworking woman, a loving wife and mother and a dependable friend and neighbor. She would be missed by all. He paused, and his message was rendered into English by the translator at his side.

Then there were words of comfort and advice from the headman to the survivors. It was fitting and proper, he said, for them to weep and mourn over the loss of Rebecca, but when the formalities were over and done with, they must go on with their lives. For everything is born, and everything must die, and the Earth itself will not live forever. He paused again for the translator to speak to those who did not understand.

Then the headman spoke of the meaning and purpose of life. He talked about how all of life is related and how all things must be kept in balance. He spoke of the different categories of life and of the necessity of keeping them separate and pure, and the translator repeated these things in English.

The headman then talked about proper human behavior and the appropriate attitude toward, not just other human beings, but all forms of life, including the earth itself. Always strive to do good, he said, for evil returns upon the perpetrator of evil. And he paused again to allow the translator to speak.

Then he prayed. He prayed for the soul of the deceased, and he prayed for strength for the survivors. He prayed for spiritual guidance for himself and for all present, and he prayed for the enlightenment of all mankind that the world might become a better place for all. And finally he prayed for the patience to endure when the ways of the universe were too mysterious for the minds of men to comprehend. The translator repeated the prayer. And then they sang.

They sang the Cherokee language version of the hymn "Amazing Grace," a song they had sung on the Trail of Tears, and then they sang the song called "One

Drop of Blood." The singing done, the headman put his hat back on his head, and the other men followed his example.

Six of the seven pallbearers then took up the coffin. They walked around the fire, moving in the same direction they had before. After they had made one complete circle, the seventh man replaced one of the others and they made the circle again. They continued in this manner until seven circles had been made around the fire and each of the seven pallbearers had been relieved of one round each. After the seventh circle, they continued walking in a straight line and left the ceremonial ground, carrying the casket, moving west.

Deputies Joe Peavy and Jake Owens rode with White Sut Beck and Bill Beck toward the home of Zeke Proctor, the old home, the one that had been the home of his parents and later the home of his recently deceased wife, Rebecca. White Sut had heard of the death of Rebecca, and he had learned the date of the planned funeral. He knew that the burial would take place there on the Proctor farm at the Proctor family cemetery.

"We ain't supposed to arrest him just yet," Peavy said. "We're supposed to wait until after the Cherokee trial. See how it comes out. You know that, don't you?"

"I know," White Sut replied.

"I guess it won't hurt anything for us to go take a look," Owens said. "If anybody says anything, you could just be paying your respects. That's all. You know them, don't you, the Proctors?"

"Yeah," Peavy said. "I know them."

"Even with all this trouble between me and Zeke," White Sut said, "he won't think nothing of me showing up for an occasion like this. Nobody would. I sure didn't wish no harm on Rebecca. She was a fine woman. Zeke knows how I feel."

The cemetery was off the road that led to Shilo, just five miles east and across the Arkansas line. When the Becks and the deputies arrived, a crowd had already gathered. Right away Joe Peavy noticed the cordon of heavily armed men surrounding the mourners, looking out, not watching the burial.

"Would you look at that," he said. "I'd say them old boys is prepared for trouble."

"They ain't taking no chances," White Sut Beck said. "That's all. They don't want nobody bothering Zeke during a time like this."

"Well, who are they?" Owens asked, his eyes wide and his mouth agape. "I don't believe I've ever seen so damn many armed Indians together in one big bunch like that. I know I ain't."

"Ah, they're friends and relatives of ol' Zeke's, I guess," Peavey said.

"They're Keetoowahs," White Sut Beck said.

"What?"

"They're members of the Keetoowah Society, and they're here to protect one of their own. Zeke's a Keetoowah. He's one of them."

"Well, what is a Ka—whatever you said?" Owens asked.

"It's a secret society of mostly full-blood Cherokees. Some say it goes way back. Farther than anyone can remember. Others say it got started right before the war. I don't know who's right about that.

"But whatever the truth is, just before the war,

53

old Evan Jones, the Baptist preacher over there at Peavine, got some of them organized as a bunch of abolitionists. That bunch called themselves Nighthawks. Sometimes they were called Pins. They fought for the Union during the war. I sure fought against them enough during that time, me and the rest of Stand Watie's Confederate Cherokees. That's where all the bad blood between us Becks and the Proctors first come from. The Civil War. Now I ain't even sure we had any business being in that war at all. It was a white man's war. It was your war. Not ours.

"Anyhow, they're still around, the Keetoowahs, and now they're supposed to be a religious organization. They claim to be upholding or reviving the old ways. I ain't real sure. There's some Creeks and Notchee Indians in amongst them too. At least, that's what I hear."

"Well, right now," Owens said, "they look to me, this bunch right here, like they're more ready to go to war than to church."

"I'm glad that we ain't supposed to serve this warrant yet," Peavy said. "I don't believe this would be a good time to try to tangle with Mr. Zeke Proctor. We'd be outnumbered and outgunned. That's for sure."

"That's for damn sure," Owens agreed.

"Well, whenever the time comes," White Sut said, "that's exactly what you'll be up against. That's what we'll all be up against."

"Let's hope that the Cherokee courts will do their job and convict him of the murder," Owens said. "Then they can hang him, and we won't have to deal with it at all."

"I don't think there's much hope of that," White

Sut said. "Lewis Downing, the current Principal Chief of the Cherokee Nation, is also a Keetoowah, and they all look out for their own."

Peavy shuddered violently from his shoulders clear down to his boots, causing his horse to jump forward and whinny.

"I'm getting the willies," he said. "Come on. Let's get the hell on out of here."

The coffin had been lowered into the freshly dug hole, and Zeke Proctor stepped forward out of the crowd. He knelt beside the grave, scooped up a handful of loose dirt, and dropped it slowly into the hole and onto the casket. Tears ran down his cheeks.

"Do-na-da-go-huh-i," he said in a low voice. "We'll see one another again."

7

Debate was heated in the chambers of the Cherokee National Council. Judge Jim Walker was a popular man and highly respected. His supporters, and there were many, maintained that nothing could keep the judge from rendering a fair decision. Besides, they said, it would be a jury trial, and the jury, not the judge, would decide on the guilt or innocence of Ezekiel Proctor.

But the Becks were a large and influential family, and, primarily through White Sut, they had applied pressure everywhere they could. And so their position was well-represented by several council members.

The judge would oversee the jury selection process, they said, and he would advise the jury. And even though the jury would render the verdict, the judge would determine the sentence. Walker was too closely associated with the Proctors. He was related to them, and he was associated with the Keetoowahs. The Becks and their supporters would not stand for it, they said. A different judge, somebody impartial, would have to be appointed.

When the debate at last ended and the vote was taken, the council decided to replace Judge Walker with someone else, someone not related to anyone on either side of the dispute.

"All right," Lewis Downing said after the issue had been decided. "Now tell me where I'm to find such a man. Tell me who to replace Judge Walker with."

"That's not our job," said the councilor from Delaware District. "The chief appoints the judges."

"I appoint and you unappoint," Downing said. "Tell me who would satisfy you, so we don't have to go through all this again."

There was a long silence in the chambers as council members scratched their heads and pondered. Then, "How about Thomas Wolf?" said the councilor from Goingsnake District. "He's a good judge. I never heard of anybody who had anything against Tom."

There was no argument. There were a few voices of assent, and one member of the council spoke at some length on the judge's behalf. His twenty-five-year career had begun with his appointment by Chief John Ross as a circuit judge back in '47.

He had served several years as clerk of the council, and he had been an associate judge on the Cherokee National Supreme Court. He was imminently qualified. There was perhaps no one in the Cherokee Nation better qualified than Judge Thomas Wolf. There could certainly be no objections to his appointment.

"All right," Downing said, hearing no objections. "Thomas Wolf it will be."

Jack Wright received the news of the appointment

of Thomas Wolf the day after the debate in the Cherokee National Council. He saddled up his horse immediately to ride out to Zeke Proctor's house and give him the news. He found Zeke working on a fence, the guards, Cull and Frog, helping.

"'*Siyo*, Jack," Zeke said. "Say, I really appreciate you sending these two boys out here to help me. It sure makes the work go faster."

"I see," Wright said. He swung down out of the saddle and wiped his forehead with the sleeve of his right arm. "It's a pretty warm day for that kind of work, ain't it?"

"Work don't know nothing about the weather," Zeke replied. "It needs doing when it needs doing. What brings you out here? Don't you trust these boys to ride herd on me?"

"The council replaced Judge Walker," Wright said. "I just found out."

"Well?" Zeke said. "You going to make me ask you who they replaced him with?"

"Tom Wolf is your new judge."

Zeke dropped his end of a fence rail to the ground and turned sharply to face the sheriff. "Tom Wolf?" he said. "They can't do that to me."

"What's wrong with Tom?" Wright asked.

"He's related to the Becks, that's all. That's what's wrong with him. They want to see me hang, and they'll put pressure on him all right. I've got to protest this. They can't let him sit on this case. He'd be prejudiced against me right from the start."

Jack Wright let out an exasperated sigh and started climbing back into his saddle.

"The chief's not going to be happy about this," he

said. "He's already called a special council meeting to replace one judge."

"He don't have to like it," Zeke replied. "He replaced that one judge because the Becks didn't want him. Well, by God, he's going to have to replace another one. That's all there is to it. It's my trial, not theirs. I guess I've got as many rights as the Becks have got."

That same day, White Sut Beck heard the same news from his brother Bill, not very long after it had reached Zeke.

"They reset the trial date and everything," Bill said. "A messenger from Tahlequah just brought the news up to Jack Wright, and I guess old Jack rode right on out to tell Zeke."

"Well, they'll just have to do it all over again," White Sut said. "Tom Wolf won't do. Not for this trial, he won't."

"What's wrong with Tom?" said Bill. "I figured he'd be on our side. He's related to us somehow or other, ain't he?"

"He ain't that close related," White Sut replied, "and he's had political appointments from Lewis Downing and even from old Chief John Ross. Union sympathizers and Keetoowahs all the way. He'd likely hold our Confederate connections against us and side with Zeke. Sometimes, Bill, politics is stronger than even family."

Lewis Downing felt like pulling out his hair. He had thought that Thomas Wolf would be the perfect selection as judge for the Zeke Proctor trial. The entire council had agreed on the appointment. And now all in one day, he had been verbally assaulted in his office by both the Becks and the Proctors. Neither side was happy with the selection. Neither side would stand for it.

White Sut Beck had come in first, and he had complained of political connections between Wolf and the Proctors. They were both pro-Union during the war, Beck had said, and everyone knew that the Becks had been Confederate. He had very carefully avoided mentioning the war activities and political leaning of the chief, but Downing knew that the sly old fox was thinking about them.

"Sut," Downing had said, "you know that's not what this trial is all about. It's not about politics, and the war's over. This is a murder trial, plain and simple."

"And you know," Beck had come back, "that there ain't nothing that plain and simple. Politics gets into everything. I'm telling you, we've got to have an unbiased judge sitting on the bench for this trial. If we don't, there's going to be bloodshed."

"Sut, don't be making threats now," Downing said.

"I ain't," White Sut replied. "I'm just telling you how it is."

Later that same day, Johnson Proctor, Zeke's brother, had come into the office.

"Chief," Johnson had said, "I come here to protest the appointment of old Tom Wolf as judge in my brother's upcoming trial. You might not have known about it, but old Tom, he's related to the Becks. I think that some kind of official protest could be made about that, don't you? Well, I don't want to do anything like that, but I thought that maybe I ought to come and talk to you about it."

Downing sat with a list in front of him on his desk. It had on it the names of all of the available Cherokee judges, and he was going over the names one at a time, trying to recall family relationships and political alliances. If he knew that a man was related to either the Becks or the Proctors, he scratched that name off the list. If he knew that a man was a strong Unionist or a strong Confederate during the late war, he scratched off that name. The names of all Keetoowahs were removed from the list.

There were several names still left, and Downing was studying them over and over, trying to call to memory everything he knew about the men. While he was thus engaged, Judge Thomas Wolf walked into the office.

"If you're all wrapped up in something," the judge said, "I can come back later."

"No, no," Downing said. "Come on in. It's the Zeke Proctor trial that's got me all wrapped up here anyway."

"Oh. What's the problem?" Wolf asked.

"Sit down," Downing said, and Wolf dragged a chair for himself over next to the chief's desk.

"What is it?" he said. "Can I help?"

"After we went to all the trouble and expense of a special council meeting to replace Judge Walker, all because of complaints from White Sut Beck, Beck and Johnson Proctor both came in here today. The Becks don't want you because of your politics, they say. The Proctors say that you're related to the Becks. I'm catching it from both sides now."

"I see," Wolf said. "Well, technically, I suppose, they're both right. Of course, one might say that since I've got reason to be prejudiced in favor of both sides, I shouldn't be prejudiced at all. But then, I'm sure that argument won't set well with either family." He thought for a moment. "Lewis," he said, "I'll make it easy for you this time. So you don't have to call the council back on this, I'll just resign."

"Well, that'll help some," the chief said. "But now, who do I appoint in your place so this same thing doesn't just happen all over again?"

"Well, let me think," Wolf said.

Downing turned around the paper he had been studying and shoved it across his desk toward Wolf.

"Here's the names of everyone who's available," he said. "I've been crossing off all those who I think either the Becks or the Proctors might have any little complaint about."

"Well then, you can cross these two off," Wolf said, pointing to two names on the list. Downing started to ask why. Instead he shrugged and crossed off the names. There were four names remaining. Wolf picked up the paper and held it in front of his face for what seemed to Downing a very long time. Then he put it down again, turned it back toward the chief and put a finger on a name.

"Right there's your best bet," he said.

Downing looked at the paper. "Cornick Sixkiller?" he said.

"Yes, sir," Wolf replied. "Blackhaw is not related to any of them, and he's about as apolitical as anybody in the entire Cherokee Nation. On top of that, he's a good judge. I can't think of a single valid complaint anyone on either side could possibly lodge against Blackhaw."

"All right then," the chief said, "it will be Cornick Sixkiller. The matter is settled, and I'll not listen to any more complaints from either side."

Two days later, White Sut Beck was back in the office of Chief Lewis Downing. The chief almost groaned aloud when he saw who was coming.

"Blackhaw Sixkiller is a friend of Zeke Proctor's," White Sut said.

"Cornick Sixkiller is liked by everyone as far as I can tell," Downing replied.

"That's not what I mean, and you know it. The two men are particular friends."

"There's no one else left," Downing said. "One side or the other will complain no matter who is appointed. I'm sorry, Sut, but it's going to have to be Judge Sixkiller. We can't keep going on like this. It just has to stop somewhere."

"That's your last word?"

"That's my last word on that subject."

"Then I'll have to go to the council with it myself," White Sut said. He was clear out in the hall when the chief stood up and called his name.

"Sut," he said. "All right. All right. Come on back in here. You don't need to go running around to council members and stirring things up. I'll call them back in, and we'll put it before them one more time."

And so the council was reconvened, and the members did not appear to be in the best of spirits. They had dealt with this issue, they thought, and had resolved it nicely enough. So now because of pressure from both the Becks and the Proctors, Judge Wolf, their choice, had resigned. The chief had appointed Judge Sixkiller, and now White Sut Beck was complaining again.

It was too much. They were disgusted. They felt as if their authority had been challenged. They felt as if their time was being infringed upon unnecessarily. They felt like teaching someone a lesson.

"Any of these judges would have been all right," said one of the members. "All of these complaints are doing nothing except delaying the trial."

"The trial date's been postponed twice now," another said.

"This trial has got to take place. What will the white man's newspapers say if they get ahold of this story?"

For once there was no argument. There was discussion, but they were all agreed. Someone at last called for the vote, and the vote was unanimous. The trial date was reset, for the last time, they said, and the presiding judge would be Cornick "Blackhaw" Sixkiller. The meeting was adjourned.

8

Zeke Proctor sat in a large rocking chair in the living room of the house that had been Rebecca's. In his lap he held all three triplets, Linnie, Willie, and Minnie. He rocked wildly, and the babies laughed. In the kitchen area, Zeke's sister Elizabeth worked at preparing what looked like enough food to feed an army. Shortly after Rebecca's untimely death, she had insisted on moving in to help Zeke with the children. Six-year-old Charlotte was doing what she could to help her aunt with the kitchen work.

Cull and Frog, still heavily and conspicuously armed, sat at the table drinking coffee. Outside, Elizabeth's two small children played with little Francis. Cull finished his coffee and stood up, moving toward the door.

"Where you going?" Frog asked.

"Oh, I think I'll just go on out and set on the porch a while," Cull replied. "Kind of keep an eye on those little ones."

"They're all right," Zeke said. "They play out there all the time."

"Maybe so," Cull said, "but I'll feel better if I go on out there and watch them."

He opened the door and stepped outside.

"I wonder what old Jack would say about that," Frog said.

"About what?" Zeke asked.

"He sent me and Cull out here to watch you, and now old Cull is watching your kids."

Zeke laughed, and, influenced by his jolly roar, the triplets all laughed with him. When the laughter died down a little, Frog moved his chair slightly and leaned forward toward Zeke.

"Zeke," he said, "there ain't going to be no trouble here today is there?"

Zeke stopped rocking and looked intently at Frog. "What are you talking about? What kind of trouble would there be?"

"You're supposed to go to trial in the morning," Frog said, "and all your folks are coming over here today. Me and Cull, we're sure going to be outnumbered here."

"Oh," Zeke said, "I get it. You think they might be coming over here to rescue me from you. Right? Well, you can stop worrying. My family's gathering up here to eat and visit and to wish me luck tomorrow. That's all. Why would anyone want to shoot you? I gave myself up to Jack Wright. Remember? I got kids around here too. I don't want no shooting around my house. If anyone tries to shoot you boys over me, it's going to be the Becks. It ain't going to be my family."

* * *

Aaron Beck sat in a rocker, a blanket draped over his lap and legs. White Sut Beck stood before a large gun cabinet laying out boxes of ammunition, checking to make sure there was plenty for each gun in the cabinet.

"You're not planning any trouble are you, Sut?" Aaron asked.

"I won't start any," White Sut replied, "but I damn sure want to be ready if someone else starts it. And they're looking for it. I know that."

"How?"

"What's that?"

"How do you know that? How do you know they're looking for trouble? And who do you mean by they? You say *they're* looking for trouble. Who are they?"

"I mean Zeke Proctor's friends, that's who I mean, starting with Chief Lewis Downing right up there at the top. I know they're looking for trouble because I learned that they've moved the place for the trial."

"The trial's tomorrow, ain't it?" the old man asked.

"It's tomorrow," White Sut said, "but it ain't going to happen at the courthouse."

"What? It ain't? Where's it going to be then?"

"Lewis Downing ordered that the trial be held at the Whitmire Schoolhouse."

"How come? We got a courthouse. That's what it's for, ain't it? What's he want to have the trial in the schoolhouse for?"

"The courthouse has too many windows," White Sut said. "The schoolhouse only has one window and one door, and it's a sturdy log house. That's what they said. That's the reason they gave for the move."

"So they are expecting trouble," Aaron said, and he started rocking fast.

"Yeah," White Sut said. "That's what I just said. I think there's another reason too. Whitmire School's farther away from here than the courthouse is. I think Downing's hoping that some of us might not bother to go all the way down there. Well, we'll be there, all right. We'll be there."

"Sut," Aaron said, "I don't want you or any other Beck starting any trouble over there. You hear me?"

"Like I said, we won't start it, but we mean to be ready for it if someone else starts it. That's all."

Johnson Proctor, with his family, was the first to arrive at his brother's house. His wife and children were in a wagon driven by the oldest boy. Johnson rode along beside the wagon on his favorite horse, a handsome gray gelding of medium size which Johnson called Reb because of its color.

Cull and Frog were on the porch, and Elizabeth was around the corner of the house to Johnson's right. She was cooking over a large fire. Charlotte was busy keeping the three smaller children away from the fire. From inside the house, Zeke had heard the approach of the wagon, and he stepped out the front door to see who was coming.

"It's your brother," Frog said. "Where're your babies?"

"I put them to bed a few minutes ago," Zeke replied. He stepped down off the porch just as Johnson rode on up close. "Get down and stay a while," he said.

"I come to eat," Johnson said. "Where's the food?"

From around the corner of the house Elizabeth called out in a loud, clear voice, "Won't be long."

Charlotte came running, abandoning her charges,

68

but they followed after her anyway. They all ran toward Johnson.

"Uncle Johnson," Charlotte said, jumping up to grab him around the neck as he bent over to meet her.

"Hello, sweetheart," Johnson said. With Charlotte's arms still around his neck, he reached out with both his arms to embrace the other children. By then the wagon had been stopped and the rest of Johnson's family had climbed down. The children then ran from Johnson to greet the rest of the visiting Proctors, and Johnson stood up to face his brother.

"You all right, Zeke?" he asked.

"Just fine. You know Cull and Frog here?"

"Yeah," Johnson said. "How you doing, boys?"

"Getting along," Cull said, looking at the six-gun that was hanging at Johnson's side.

Frog nodded. "Johnson," he said.

"I guess we must be early," Johnson said.

"You're the first ones here," Zeke replied. "Someone's got to be first." He sat down on the edge of the porch, and Johnson sat beside him.

"Well," Johnson said, "you about ready to face them in the morning?"

"Sure, I'm ready," Zeke replied. "All I can do is tell them the truth. Tell them what I done and how it happened. I don't have to do nothing to get ready for that."

"What about the Becks?" Johnson asked.

"What about them?"

"You think they'll try anything?"

"You mean start some trouble at the trial?"

"Or somewhere in between here and there."

"Why should they?" Zeke asked. "They'd be happy to see me hang. They'll wait to see how the trial comes

69

out. If I'm found guilty of murder, they'll be satisfied."

Johnson stared at the ground for a long, silent moment.

"What if you're acquitted?" he said.

"Then we better watch out for the Becks."

"And if they find you guilty," Cull said from behind the backs of the two brothers, "then do we have to watch out for you Proctors?"

Johnson turned to look at Cull over his shoulder.

"I ain't going to stand by and watch my brother hang," he said. "Would you?"

"Well," Frog replied, "it sounds to me like we're looking for a fight after the trial no matter which way it goes."

"Sounds like," Cull said.

"Hey," Zeke said, "relax. The trial ain't even started yet. This is my home, and everyone here is my guest. I want everyone to have a good time."

"Even them two lawmen?" Johnson asked.

"Especially them," Zeke said, and he gave his brother a look to show that he meant it. Johnson shrugged.

"Hell," he said, "I reckon if White Sut Beck rode up here, you'd shake his hand and feed him."

"I would," Zeke said. "I never yet sent a human being away from my house hungry."

"And tomorrow?"

"Tomorrow we go to court."

"And after the trial?"

"After the trial, we'll see."

Just then another wagon appeared, coming down the lane toward the house. The driver was Charley Allen, married to Zeke's other sister, Rachel; and the passengers, other than Rachel, were Jane Harlan, her two Harlan children, and four-year-old Zeke Proctor, Jr. The conversation at the porch came to an abrupt halt, to be replaced by more greetings all around.

Then there was a steady stream of visitors arriving. Third sister, Nannie, and her husband Abraham Sixkiller came. The women all tended to gather around Elizabeth and the fire, and they all pitched in to help with the cooking. Most of them had brought along some kind of food to contribute to the gathering. The children ran around laughing and screaming, playing their children's games a respectable distance away from the adults.

More people came, and they ate and visited, and the children ran and played until well after the sun had gone down. Then some began to leave, a few at a time. But some had planned to stay the night in order to leave early the next morning to ride along with Zeke to the Whitmire School. Among those was Johnson Proctor.

"You going to ride in with me in the morning, huh?" Zeke asked.

"I'll ride right alongside you, Zeke," Johnson said. "I always will. You know that."

White Sut Beck was about to put out the lamp and go to bed when he heard the sound of a horse outside approaching fast. He picked up a loaded shotgun and stepped out onto his porch. The horse slowed as it came closer.

"Who is it?" White Sut called out.

"It's Bill Hicks," came the answer, and a moment later the horse and rider were close enough for White Sut to recognize Hicks.

"Climb on down, Bill," White Sut said. "What are you traveling so fast for?"

Hicks swung down off his horse's back, panting heavily.

"I was hoping to get here before you went to bed," he said. "I don't like to disturb you."

"What's this all about then?"

"I just found out," Hicks said. "There was a big gathering over there at Zeke Proctor's place this evening. I guess there's some still over there. Spending the night."

"What's wrong with that?"

"All the men was toting guns. It looked like an army over there. That's what I heard."

"You think they're going like that to the trial?"

"What else, Sut? You going to the trial?"

"You damn right I'm going."

"Well, who's going with you?"

"Sam and Bill's going," White Sut replied. "And Jim Kesterson. And those two deputies that's been hanging around."

"I'll see if I can't round up a few more," Hicks said, "and we'll ride along too. Just in case. I think old Riley Woods will go with us, and George Selvedge. Maybe Jim Ward."

"That's fine," White Sut said. "Thank you. Times like these, a man finds out who his real friends are. I appreciate it. Thanks for coming by."

"You got plenty of friends, Sut," Hicks said. "You'll see. We'll be here in the morning to ride in with you."

"Make it early," White Sut said. "You know, the chief moved the trial over to the Whitmire School."

"Yeah, I heard," Hicks said. "We'll be here plenty early. And we'll all bring our guns."

Hicks climbed back into the saddle and turned his horse to ride away.

"Good night, Sut," he said.

"Till morning," White Sut said. "And Bill, thanks again."

As Hicks rode off into the darkness, White Sut Beck stood on his porch alone wondering what the events of the next day would bring. At last he turned to go back inside. Whatever happens, he thought, whatever it is, we'll be ready. Me and my family and friends. We'll be ready.

9

April 15, 1872

Zeke Proctor rode his big black stallion, and right beside him, to his right, Johnson rode on Reb. Cull rode to Johnson's right, Frog on the left of Zeke. They rode up to the Whitmire Schoolhouse, in a clearing across the road from the home of Widow Whitmire and her thirteen-year-old son Eli. A large crowd was already gathered there. Zeke and his companions dismounted and headed for the building.

As they approached the door, Zeke noticed Sheriff Jack Wright standing there with John Walkingstick, Lincoln England, John Looney, and Jesse Shill. They were all heavily armed.

"You got yourself a pretty heavy guard here, Jack," Zeke said.

"Yeah," Wright replied. "And there's more inside."

"Why so many? You expecting trouble here today?"

"You're a prisoner of the Cherokee Nation, Zeke," the sheriff said. "We mean to see that everyone here respects that fact. That's all."

Zeke nodded and walked on through the door. The little schoolhouse was packed with spectators. At the far end of the room behind a long table and facing the door sat Judge Cornick Sixkiller, known as Blackhaw. On Sixkiller's left hand side sat Joe Starr, the court clerk. Moses Alberty, Zeke's lawyer, was seated on the judge's right. Next to him was an empty chair. When he saw Zeke come into the room, Alberty stood up and motioned to him.

"Come on up here, Zeke," he said.

Zeke made his way to the front of the room, and Alberty gestured toward the empty chair.

"Sit down here," he said, and Zeke sat down. He noticed that Tom Walkingstick, heavily armed, stood against the wall behind him, obviously another of Jack Wright's guards.

"'Siyo, Tom," he said.

"'Siyo,'" Walkingstick said.

Zeke looked out over the crowd that had gathered in the schoolhouse. He saw his brother Johnson leaning against the wall near the door. The chairs had all been taken before they had arrived. That explained the large number of people milling about outside. There was no more room in the schoolhouse.

He saw several of his friends in the crowd, mostly Keetoowahs, including Watt Christie and his son Ned, and he saw a number of others that had come, he supposed, for the entertainment value of the proceedings. As far as Zeke could tell, they had no real interest in the trial or its outcome. He did not see Cull or Frog. They must have stayed outside, he thought.

He was surprised, though, to see no Becks, no Beck relatives, no Beck friends. He couldn't believe that they had chosen to stay away. He wondered where they could be and what they might be up to. Was it possible that they had not gotten the word about the date and place of the trial? He could hardly believe that either.

Blackhaw Sixkiller turned his face toward Joe Starr. "Is everyone here now?" he asked.

"Yes, sir, I believe so," Starr replied.

"Is it time to start?"

Starr pulled a watch out of a vest pocket and consulted it.

"Yes, sir, it is," he said, and he tucked the watch back into the pocket.

"Then call the court to order," Sixkiller said.

Starr stood up, called for order and announced that the court was in session. He then identified the case before the court as the Cherokee Nation versus Ezekiel Proctor, and read the indictment against Zeke for the killing of Polly Beck Hildebrand. The judge then allowed Johnson Spake, the prosecutor, to make his opening statement.

Spake said that he intended to prove murder against Zeke, that Zeke had committed an atrocious crime, the killing of a woman. He said that Zeke had gone to the Hildebrand Mill with murder in his heart and that he had meant to kill both James Kesterson and Polly Hildebrand. Kesterson had barely escaped with his life, Spake said, running away with Zeke's bullets hitting all around him as he fled. When he had finished, Judge Sixkiller called on Moses Alberty.

"My worthy opponent," Alberty said, "is an impassioned and skillful orator, but unfortunately he has got his facts all wrong. The truth is plain and simple. My client, Ezekiel Proctor, went to the mill to confront Mr. James Kesterson for good reason. Mr.

76

Kesterson was married, technically still is married, to Mr. Proctor's sister Elizabeth. Mr. Kesterson abandoned his wife and two small children, leaving them to fend for themselves. That is the matter about which Mr. Proctor went to see Mr. Kesterson.

"In the course of their conversation, Mr. Kesterson went for his gun. Mr. Proctor, responding in self-defense, drew out his own revolver and fired it. Just at that crucial point, Mrs. Hildebrand stepped in the way and was killed. Mr. Proctor fired in self-defense. The death of Mrs. Hildebrand was an accident. I expect to hear a verdict of not guilty."

There were some murmurs in the courtroom, and Cornick Sixkiller rapped the table with his gavel.

"I expect to have order in this courtroom," he said in a loud voice. "If there are any disturbances, I will have the sheriff clear the courtroom." He raised his voice even more. "And that goes for those of you outside hanging around the door too. I consider you to be in my court. If you can't keep quiet, I'll have you moved away and have the door shut."

Outside, the people at the back of the crowd were the first to be aware of the approach of the Becks, and in spite of the judge's admonishment, a new murmur moved through their ranks like windswept prairie grass.

White Sut Beck was riding directly toward the people gathered around the door, and he was flanked by the two federal deputy marshals. Behind them were Sam Beck, Bill Beck, Black Sut Beck, and John Beck, brother of the unfortunate Polly. Then came William Hicks, Riley Woods, George Selvedge, and James Ward. James Kesterson brought up the rear. It was a formidable posse, and as its members dismounted, the people who were massed around the door of the schoolhouse automatically moved aside, creating an aisle for them to walk through.

White Sut Beck was the first to walk to the door, and he was met there by Jack Wright, who deliberately barred his way.

"Sut," he said, "leave your weapons outside. I don't mean to have no trouble here."

"We've got federal law with us, Jack," White Sut said.

"Federal law's got no business here," the sheriff replied.

Inside the schoolhouse the procedure of the court had stopped. Judge Sixkiller and everyone else had their eyes on the open door.

"Step out of the way, Jack," White Sut said, and he raised a double-barreled shotgun which he had been holding down at his side. He pointed the gun at the sheriff's chest and pulled back both hammers. Jack Wright looked White Sut in the face for an instant, then stepped out of the doorway. White Sut walked in, and George Blackwood, a member of the jury, stood up and pointed.

"Look out!" he shouted. "They're coming to get Zeke Proctor!"

White Sut was still holding the gun up in a firing position, and Johnson Proctor, standing just inside the door, jumped quickly in front of White Sut and grabbed the barrel of the gun. White Sut pulled one trigger, and the shotgun roared. There were shouts and screams from those gathered there as Johnson, his guts ripped out, with his last strength shoved the shotgun barrel toward the floor. As he collapsed,

White Sut pulled the other trigger. The blast went into the floor, and shot skittered toward the other end of the room. Zeke was diving to one side, and some of the stray shot buried itself in his thigh.

He yelled and grabbed Tom Walkingstick's revolver before Walkingstick could react. Raising the gun, Zeke fired a shot at White Sut, and the slug tore into White Sut's left shoulder. Sam Beck stepped protectively in front of White Sut, raised his own shotgun and fired both barrels. Moses Alberty took both shots in the chest. He jerked backward, then fell forward over the table, dead, leaking a tremendous amount of blood onto the tabletop to run down onto the floor.

Zeke fired again, hitting Sam Beck in the chest. Sam stood swaying for a moment, dropped the shotgun and pitched forward on his face. Zeke's third shot tore through White Sut's side. Hands grabbed the wounded Beck from behind and dragged him back out the door.

Seeing that the Becks were moving back outside, Zeke ran for the nearby window. As he was climbing out, someone fired a shot. The bullet struck him just below his knee. He threw himself out and onto the ground. Rolling over, he came to his feet and ran, limping for the front of the schoolhouse.

As he rounded the building, he saw Lincoln England shoot Black Sut Beck in the chest. He saw Bill Hicks firing from outside back into the courtroom through the open door. He pointed his "borrowed" revolver and fired, hitting Hicks in the side of the head.

Then the Becks were moving back toward their horses, firing as they went. Jack Wright and his deputies, aided by Zeke Proctor, were still close to the schoolhouse door, firing from there. George Selvedge, running toward his horse, staggered, hit twice. He painfully pulled himself into the saddle and started to ride away, but he had not gone far when he fell to the ground. The horse ran on alone.

Jim Ward stopped about halfway to the horses and turned to fire back at the sheriff and his deputies. Three or four shots hit him, and he fell in his tracks. Then in a final desperate effort, what was left of the Becks all turned and fired back at the schoolhouse door.

Isaac Vann, standing beside Zeke, yelled in pain and dropped his gun as a bullet smashed his elbow, and Andrew Palone fell dead with a bullet in his heart.

Joe Peavy took the reins of White Sut's horse and kicked his own in the sides.

"Hang on," he shouted. "We got to get the hell out of here."

White Sut Beck, hanging onto the saddle horn, allowed himself to be led away. He was bleeding badly from his two wounds and swaying dangerously in the saddle, but somehow he managed to keep his seat.

Then suddenly, as suddenly as it had started, it was over. The Becks who were left alive were gone. Jack Wright ran toward his horse, calling his deputies over his shoulder.

"Come on," he said. "Let's get them."

Wright was soon on the trail, followed close by the two Walkingsticks and Lincoln England. Zeke limped around the yard looking over the carnage. Then he remembered Johnson, and he hobbled into the school-house. There, inside the door, was his brother's body.

Zeke knelt down beside it and lifted Johnson's head to cradle it in his lap. Slowly he began to rock back and forth, and quietly he hummed a doleful tune.

Judge Blackhaw Sixkiller stepped up to stand beside him. The judge's right arm was hanging limp at his side, blood running freely from two bullet wounds in the wrist and hand.

Outside, the widow Whitmire was shouting orders. She started with her own son, young Eli.

"Get over to the house and get the wagon," she said. "Bring it here. Hurry up now!"

She had the injured taken to her house, where she personally tended to their wounds. Then, when there was nothing more to be done for the living, the bodies of the dead were brought to the house and laid out on the front porch. Riders were sent out to notify the next of kin of all the dead and wounded. And about that time, Wright and his deputies returned.

"They got across the line into Arkansas," Wright said. "What do we have here?"

Jesse Shill, one of the deputies who had not gone with Wright in pursuit of Beck, answered him.

"We got ten killed," he said. "Two more is like to die, including one of them federal marshals—I don't know his name. Also several wounded, including the judge."

"Who's dead?" Wright asked.

"Johnson Proctor, John Beck, Mose Alberty, Sam Beck, Andy Palone, Black Sut Beck, Bill Hicks, Jim Ward, George Selvedge, and Riley Woods."

Wright stood amazed. He shook his head in disbelief. "I wouldn't have thought it could happen," he said. "I thought that White Sut Beck had more sense than that. There wasn't no sense in all this. No sense in it at all. These people didn't have to be killed. God, this is the worst thing I ever seen."

"It was pretty stupid," Shill said.

"Why did he do it?" Wright asked. "Why?"

He got no answer, but just then Judge Sixkiller came walking out of the house. His right hand was bandaged. He stepped toward the sheriff.

"Jack," he said, "this trial has got to be concluded as quickly as possible. Get ahold of everyone who needs to be there. Only those who need to be there, no one else. You understand?"

"I sure do, Judge," Wright replied.

"Tell them that court will reconvene at eight o'clock in the morning at Arch Scraper's house."

"Eight o'clock at Arch Scraper's house. I'll tell them."

"Jack, keep it as quiet as you can. We don't need anything like this to happen again, and we don't need any federal lawmen around to try to interfere."

10

Sheriff Jack Wright had spoken to everyone he needed to concerning the new time and place for the trial. One juror had been wounded and would have to be replaced, but the judge had said that he would take care of that matter himself. Judge Sixkiller had chosen the home of Arch Scraper to use as his next courtroom because it was nearby and because Scraper was foreman of the jury. And Scraper had readily agreed. Sixkiller was determined to get this trial concluded.

Wright was standing in the yard in front of the Whitmire house, feeling numb and useless, when he saw a rider approaching from down the road. He wrinkled his face against the sun and watched as the rider moved closer. Soon he recognized William Penn Boudinot, the editor of the *Cherokee Advocate*.

Boudinot rode on up close to the house and dismounted. He walked slowly toward the house, a look of astonishment on his face.

"My God, Jack," he said, "what has happened here?"

"You don't know?" Wright asked. "What are you doing here, then?"

"I came out to report on the trial. What's happened?"

"A massacre," the sheriff replied. "The worst thing I ever seen."

"Who was involved? Becks and Proctors?"

"Yeah. And a couple of federal lawmen, deputy marshals from Fort Smith. One of them is in there dying, I think."

"Will you take me in to see him?" the newspaperman asked.

"Come on," Wright said. He led the way into the Whitmire home, which had by this time undergone a transformation into a makeshift field hospital. Wounded were everywhere. Everything seemed to be covered with blood. Mrs. Whitmire bustled about still trying to attend to everyone's needs, still shouting at Eli when she required his help.

"Eli, put on some more water to boil!"

"Eli, fetch some more bandages!"

"Eli, hold this here for me!"

Wright gestured toward a doorway that led into a separate room, a small bedroom, Boudinot figured.

"He's in there," the sheriff said.

They walked into the bedroom, and Boudinot saw two men lying side by side in the bed. Both men were bandaged, and the bandages were all bloodsoaked. Both men appeared to be near death.

"This here is Deputy U.S. Marshal Jake Owens," said Wright, motioning to the man nearest to them. Owens rolled his eyes toward the two men.

"Who's the other one?" Boudinot asked.

"That's Bill Beck."

Beck did not appear to have any interest in matters of this earth. If he was conscious, he was barely so. Wright spoke to Owens.

"Deputy Owens," he said, "I brought Mr. Boudinot here in to see you. He's the editor of the Cherokee Nation's newspaper."

"I thought that you might have something to say about all this, Mr. Owens," Boudinot said. "I thought I should give you the chance."

"I tried to stop them," Owens said. His voice was weak, and Boudinot and Wright had to strain to hear. "I told him not to carry that shotgun up to the door. I tried, but they wouldn't listen to me."

"Mr. Owens," Boudinot said, "you were here with a partner, were you?"

"Joe Peavy. Yeah. That's right. I came with Joe. Where is Joe? Is Joe all right?"

Boudinot looked toward the sheriff for help.

"Peavy's all right, as far as I know," the sheriff said. "He rode out of here leading White Sut Beck away to safety, I guess. Beck was hurt, pretty bad, I think, but I don't think Peavy had so much as a scratch. We chased them, but they got on across the line into Arkansas. They were headed into Cincinnati."

"Mr. Owens," Boudinot said, "why were you and Mr. Peavy here in the first place? What was the interest of the United States in a case that was clearly within the jurisdiction of the Cherokee Nation?"

"We had a warrant for the arrest of Zeke Proctor," Owens said.

"But both Zeke and Mrs. Hildebrand were Cherokee citizens," Boudinot said. "It's a Cherokee case, and the trial was in progress."

"Our warrant was for assault on a white man—Jim Kesterson," Owens replied. "We weren't supposed to serve it unless the court let Proctor go. He couldn't wait. White Sut Beck just couldn't wait. I told him. I tried to stop it. I did."

"Yes. I'm sure you did your best, Mr. Owens," Boudinot said. "You rest now. I think we've bothered you long enough. Try to get some rest."

Owens smiled a wry and weak half smile.

"I don't reckon I need to rest in order to die," he said.

Wright and Boudinot went back outside. Boudinot sat down on the edge of the porch and made some notes on a pad he carried with him. Wright looked at the bodies lined up there. He thought that it seemed a bit callous to relax beside the recently dead. He looked around, but he could think of no place to go, nothing that he had to do right then. He was about to give it up and sit down beside Boudinot when he saw the two Walkingsticks with Zeke Proctor coming toward him from the schoolhouse across the road. He walked out to meet them, and they came together and stopped in the middle of the road.

"Zeke," Wright said, "you might as well go on home now. There's no need for you to hang around here any longer." He turned toward Tom Walkingstick. "You two boys can stay with him. Can't you? Bring him to court in the morning?"

"Sure," Tom said. "We'll stay with Zeke."

"We'll come with him in the morning too," John said.

"I'll have to come right back here with a wagon for my brother," Zeke said.

"Yeah," Wright replied. "Of course. You two stay with him. And listen here. I trust Zeke. I ain't afraid that he's going to try to run away. That ain't why you're going with him. You know what I mean? Be careful. Keep your eyes peeled."

Zeke limped toward the horses, the two Walkingsticks right behind him. When they reached the horses, Zeke mounted his black stallion, then reached down to untie the reins of Reb.

"Right beside me," he said, and as the three men rode down the lane, Zeke led the saddled but riderless Reb along beside him.

Boudinot had gotten a narrative of the events at Whitmire School from Sheriff Jack Wright, and he had taken several pages of notes. He had listed the names of the dead and dying, and named as many of the wounded as he could get names for. He stopped writing and looked back over his notes. John Looney, one of Wright's deputies, had strolled over and was standing nearby.

"Let me just check a few details here, Jack," Boudinot said. "You said that the trial had already started, and you were standing at the door with some of your deputies."

"That's right," the sheriff replied.

"White Sut Beck came up, and behind him were Sam Beck, Bill Beck, John Beck, Black Sut Beck, William Hicks, Riley Woods, George Selvedge, and James Ward. Is that correct?"

"Yeah, as far as I can remember."

"Jim Kesterson was with them," Looney said.

"Oh, yeah," the sheriff said, "that's right. He was there. I remember now. What happened to him anyway?"

"He run for tall timber soon as the first shot was fired," Looney replied. "I seen him go."

For the rest of that day, wagons rolled in, one after another, carrying people with long, sad faces, coming to take away their dead. Sounds of weeping, moaning, and keening filled the air. Jack Wright stayed until the last body had been removed and the last of the wounded had either gone home on his own or been picked up by friends or relatives, the last but two.

Jake Owens and Bill Beck still clung to life. They were dying, almost for sure, but they were taking their time about it. Wright sat down on the edge of the porch. With the bodies gone, it did not seem so bad. His legs and his back were tired and aching. He heard the door open behind him and looked over his shoulder to see Mrs. Whitmire stepping out.

"Jack," she said, "you look beat."

"I am, but I'll be all right," he said. "You've been going pretty hard yourself."

"Oh, I'm doing fine. I just wish I could do more. Why don't you go on home, Jack? There's nothing more you can do here. I'll keep those two in there as comfortable as I can, but I'm afraid that's all I can do for them. I don't think they'll last much longer."

Wright stood up and stretched.

"Well," he said, "maybe you're right. Maybe I will head on home. I know I'm going to have to write up a long report about what happened out here. They'll probably want it in Tahlequah tomorrow. I'll leave a couple of deputies here with you until—well, you know."

"Run along, Jack. Get yourself some rest and get your report wrote. We'll be all right out here."

Zeke Proctor stopped that night at the home of Jane Harlan. He had already taken the body of Johnson back to his family, and he had spent some time with them. He had gone to his other home and spent time with his and Rebecca's children and with his sister Elizabeth and her two little ones. He wanted to go see the family of Moses Alberty, but the Alberty home was too far away, and there wasn't enough time to make the trip. It would have to wait until tomorrow. At such a time, with so much grief, there were too many places he needed to be.

But at last he considered his own needs, and he went to see Jane. It was late by the time Zeke reached the house, and the children were already in bed. The two Walkingsticks waited outside on the porch. Jane made some fresh coffee, after seeing that Zeke was as comfortable as possible, his wounded leg propped up on a hassock.

"You heard about what happened?" Zeke said.

"News like that travels fast," she said. "I'm sorry about Johnson. Real sorry. We're all going to miss him."

Zeke swallowed hard and fought back a tear.

"He said he'll always ride beside me," he told her. "He died for me. White Sut Beck meant to shoot me, and Johnson stepped in front of the gun. He took the shot that White Sut meant for me."

He paused to take several deep breaths, and Jane brought him a cup of hot coffee. He reached out and

89

took it in his right hand, but he continued to stare straight ahead.

"White Sut Beck," he said.

"Zeke," Jane said, "are you thinking about going after him?"

"He killed my brother."

"Let the law handle it," Jane said.

"The law was handling things this morning," he replied, "and you heard what happened over there. There's ten men dead, and one of them is my brother."

"But where does it end, Zeke? You killed Polly. I know you didn't mean to, but you did. White Sut came after you for that, and he killed Johnson. Just like you, he didn't mean to, but he did it."

"He meant to kill me," Zeke said.

"I know, but it's got to stop somewhere. If you kill him, then one of these days some other Beck will get you. It's bound to happen. And if you don't care about your own self, what about your son? Is Zeke, Junior, going to have to kill Becks when he grows up? Or is some Beck going to kill him? Or little Willie. What about little Willie? Zeke, it can't go on. It can't go on like this."

Zeke sipped from his coffee cup, then rested it on the right arm of the big chair in which he sat. Jane moved to his left side and perched herself on the armrest. She took his head with her right hand and pulled it to her, and he closed his eyes. He thought about what she had said. He knew it made sense.

And what she had said made him recall some of his own earlier thoughts. He thought again about the killing of Polly Beck, and he realized with a kind of quiet horror that he, himself, might well be responsible for the death of Johnson. Polly. Rebecca. Johnson. All things must balance out, one way or another.

"Jane, darling," he said, "of course you're right. It's hard, but you're right about it. I won't go after White Sut Beck. I promise you."

Jane smiled and slipped off the arm of the chair. Then she leaned over and kissed Zeke tenderly.

"You're a good man, Zeke Proctor," she said. "I never knew a better. Right now I better take some coffee out to those men we left out on the porch."

"No," said Zeke. "Tell them to come on inside. We'll stay here tonight."

11

Without White Sut to lead them, the Becks failed to regroup, and as a result they did not discover the new time and place of the trial. Probably they did not expect such quick action on the part of Judge Cornick Sixkiller immediately following such a disastrous day in court.

At any rate, the trial was speedy and clean. Whether the judge and jury actually believed that the death of Polly Beck Hildebrand was accidental and that Zeke was, therefore, not responsible for it, or, because of the violence they had all experienced the day before they had chosen sides in the Beck-Proctor feud and their verdict was a reflection of their allegiance, no one could say. But even Spake had tempered his prosecutorial orations.

It was like a routine ritual endured by one and all solely for the sake of rubber stamping a foregone conclusion. The jury said not guilty, and the judge dismissed the case. Zeke was released from custody.

"Does that mean our jobs are over?" Tom Walkingstick asked Jack Wright.

"Your jobs are over," the sheriff replied. "Go on home or wherever you want to go."

"I think we'll go along with Zeke," Tom said.

"Yeah. Me too," John said. "Zeke might get lonesome or something."

Before he finally arrived at his own house, Zeke found himself accompanied by not only the two Walkingsticks, but also by Lincoln England, John Looney, Jesse Shill, his brother-in-law Charley Allen, and three relatives of the judge—Soldier, One, and Redbird Sixkiller. All of those men were Keetoowahs. In the middle of this small army of self-appointed protectors, Zeke rode his black stallion and led the gray gelding at his left side. The trial was over. But the ordeal had just begun.

Judge Sixkiller was not the only one to react quickly to the incident at the Whitmire School. The trial at Arch Scraper's house was barely over when a band of twenty men rode up to the Whitmire School. They quickly took in the situation there and crossed the street to the Whitmire home. Mrs. Whitmire stepped out onto the porch.

"Who are you?" she demanded. "What do you want here?"

The leader of the group swung down out of his saddle and approached Mrs. Whitmire.

"I'm a deputy U.S. marshal, ma'am," he said. "C. F. Robinson's my name. I've got two doctors with me here. Do you have any wounded that needs tending to?"

"They've all been tended and gone home," said Mrs. Whitmire. "All except them that died."

"Is Ezekiel Proctor anywhere on the premises?"

"He's gone. They're all gone."

"I have a list of names here," Robinson said, reaching into his inside coat pocket, "of men that are wanted by the United States." He began to read from the paper in his hands. "Mr. Ezekiel Proctor, Mr. Jesse Shill, Mr. Soldier Sixkiller, Mr. One Sixkiller, Mr. Thomas Walkingstick, Mr. John Creek, Mr. John Proctor, Mr. Ellis Foreman, Mr. Isaac Vann, Mr. Joe Chaney, and the entire jury that was impaneled to try Mr. Proctor. These men are wanted in connection with the attack on two deputy United States marshals, Deputies Peavy and Owens. Are any of these named persons anywhere on the premises?"

"No, they ain't," Mrs. Whitmire said. "I done told you that everyone's gone."

"Do you know the whereabouts of any of these named persons?"

"I can only tell you two things," Mrs. Whitmire said. "If you want to arrest Johnson Proctor, you'll have to arrest a corpse. From what I can tell, he was the first man killed. He was shot to death at close range by White Sut Beck with a shotgun, and Johnson was unarmed too."

"That remains for the court to decide," Robinson said.

"The court don't decide whether or not Johnson was armed," Mrs. Whitmire said. "I seen him, and he didn't have no weapons on him, and that's all there is to it."

Robinson heaved an exasperated-sounding sigh and indicated that he was anxious to get on with it.

"By the way," Mrs. Whitmire continued, "Zeke Proctor rode off from Arch Scraper's house a little while ago with fifty armed Pin Indians around him. If you go after him, you're going to have another big fight on your hands."

Robinson had no way of knowing that Mrs. Whitmire had exaggerated the truth in regards to the number of men in Zeke's armed escort, and he had no intention of fighting fifty Indians with a posse of twenty men. He decided to ride into Tahlequah instead for a visit with the chief of the Cherokee Nation.

Lewis Downing greeted Robinson formally as a representative of a foreign government.

"What can I do for you, Mr. Robinson?" he said.

Robinson reached again for the letter in his pocket. He unfolded it as he spoke. "I'm sure you've heard about the events that occurred at the Whitmire School yesterday," he said, "at the trial of Ezekiel Proctor."

"Yes, I have," the chief replied, "and it's my understanding that they would not have happened had not a posse of federal officers attempted to interfere in a matter that was purely Cherokee."

"I wouldn't know about that," Robinson said. "That's for the courts to decide."

"Whose courts, Mr. Robinson? Yours or ours?"

"I would imagine that the matter will have to be decided in the federal courts. An officer of the United States has been murdered. I have a written request to present to you on this matter."

Robinson handed the letter to Chief Downing, and the chief turned his back on the deputy while he read.

Dear Sir:

I have the honor to demand the surrender of the following named citizens of the Cherokee

Nation. Said parties were concerned in the attack made on Deputy United States Marshals J. G. Owens and Peavy, and their posse comitatus, at Goingsnake District courthouse: Jesse Shill, Ezekiel Proctor, Soldier Sixkiller, One Sixkiller, Thomas Walkingstick, John Creek, John Proctor, Isaac Vann, Ellis Foreman, Joe Chaney, and the jury that was impaneled to try Ezekiel Proctor.

> Yours very respectifully,
> Charles F. Robinson
> Deputy U.S. Marshal

Finished reading the curious letter, Downing folded it, turned back around to face Robinson, and dropped the letter on his desk.

"Mr. Robinson," he said, "this letter—signed, I presume, by you—is not an official document. I see no reason to give it an official response. I will, however, give you the courtesy of an unofficial reaction to your request.

"First of all, I do not believe that the 'posse comitatus' to which you refer was a properly constituted posse. Aside from your two deputies, it was made up of Becks, a family at odds with the Proctors and with a particular interest in the outcome of the trial.

"In the second place, from the information I have received regarding the violence at the courthouse, it would seem that the shooting was begun by the so-called posse, and that Mr. Proctor and whoever else was involved in returning fire were acting in self-defense.

"Third, I cannot imagine how you arrived at the names on your list. I have been unable to determine any details regarding the shootings, other than the apparent fact that the first shot, the shot that killed Mr. Johnson Proctor, whom you wish to arrest, was fired by White Sut Beck with no provocation.

"Finally, I resent this attempt by the federal government of the United States to interfere with matters of purely domestic concern to the Cherokee Nation, and I can assure you, Mr. Robinson, that the government of the Cherokee Nation will not cooperate in any way with such a blatant attempt at infringement on our rightful jurisdiction."

"Chief, I don't want to argue with you," Robinson said, "but this whole matter first came up when Mr. Ezekiel Proctor attempted murder on a white man. James Kesterson filed charges against Mr. Proctor in Fort Smith. Now you should know as well as I do that when an Indian assaults a white man, even within the boundaries of your nation, that is a federal matter."

"I believe," the chief said, "if you'll look again at the law, Mr. Robinson, you'll find that it has nothing to do with race. I think you'll find that the laws of your United States maintain that when a citizen of the Cherokee Nation commits a crime against a person who is not a citizen of the Cherokee Nation, then the United States assumes jurisdiction over the case. Mr. Kesterson had married a Cherokee woman in order to obtain citizenship rights in the Cherokee Nation. When he did that, I believe he relinquished his rights as a citizen of the United States."

"Look, Chief—"

"That is my position, Mr. Robinson," Downing

said. "It will not change, and this interview is at an end."

A disgruntled Charles Robinson led his posse back to Arkansas. He was not ready, on his own decision, to start a war with the Cherokee Nation.

What immediately followed the trial for Zeke Proctor was a series of funerals. First came that of Johnson Proctor. It was conducted by officials of the Keetoowah Society much in the manner of Rebecca's so recent one. And, as before, a small Keetoowah army stood guard to make sure that Zeke would not be disturbed in his grief by lawmen from the United States.

Then came the funeral of Moses Alberty. This one was conducted in a Cherokee Baptist church, and Zeke attended. He did what he could to comfort the widow and children of his former attorney, and he assured Mrs. Alberty that as long as he lived, she and her family would never want for anything that was in his power to supply.

Finally Zeke attended the Keetoowah funeral of Andrew Palone. Then, all of a sudden, they were over. He tried to get back into the routine of work and put all of the grim events of the recent past out of his mind. But he could not put those things aside.

The bloody images from the recent schoolhouse carnage were too fresh, too vivid. There had been too much violence, too many deaths, and there was still the potential for more violence and death yet to come.

White Sut Beck had been severely wounded, but he would recover, and Zeke knew the man well enough to know that Beck would not forget. And even if White Sut did not recover sufficiently to be a threat to him and his family, other Becks would certainly carry on the pattern of revenge.

But the Becks were not the major concern in the mind of Zeke Proctor, for a federal lawman had been killed, and Zeke, along with several of his friends, had been accused. The federal marshals, he figured, would be coming after him, sooner or later, and once they got started, they wouldn't quit.

So Zeke's habits changed. He seldom went anyplace alone, but if he did, he never returned home by the same route he had taken away from home. He kept his back to a wall unless he was surrounded by his friends. And he always led the riderless gray gelding, Reb, wherever he went.

People began to tell stories about Zeke. He was the deadliest man with a gun in the Cherokee Nation and probably all of western Arkansas. He had killed his first man at the age of seven while coming west along the Trail of Tears. They said that he wore underneath his shirt a metal breastplate. Some said that Zeke had supernatural powers and a horse that was trained to sense danger and warn him of its approach.

And while the wild tales were circulating, Zeke was at home running his three farms, raising his two families and his sister's children, and doing all he could to care for the Albertys. But friends of his, Keetoowahs, almost always heavily armed, seemed to spend a great deal of time just hanging around.

Across the line in Cincinnati, Arkansas, White Sut Beck lay in the home of a friend recuperating from his wounds. He had nothing on his hands but time, nothing to do but think. He grieved silently and alone for his lost relatives and friends, and he suffered from the thought that his own actions had precipitated the violence that had taken their lives. Yet he alternated from blaming himself to blaming Zeke Proctor. Perhaps it was all the fault of Zeke Proctor.

If Zeke had not killed Polly, he told himself, none of this would have happened. Aaron had told White Sut to let the law handle Zeke, yet the law had all been stacked in Zeke's favor. White Sut had gone to the trial knowing that Chief Downing, a Keetoowah, had appointed the judge, Blackhaw Sixkiller, another Keetoowah, and that Sixkiller had selected the jurors. He had known all that, and yet he had meant to wait, to give the law a chance to do the right thing.

But when he had arrived at the Whitmire School, a place the chief had selected because he anticipated a fight—what other reason could there have been?— and he had seen the doorway guarded there by Jack Wright and his deputies, all of whom were friends of Zeke Proctor, he had suddenly lost all of his patience. He had taken the shotgun to the door with him, and when Wright had tried to bar his way, he had threatened the sheriff. Then he had stepped inside, the shotgun still held up as if ready to fire, and Johnson Proctor had reacted to the shotgun.

As he lay there in pain and deep in thought, White Sut Beck tried to blame Zeke Proctor. He tried to blame Lewis Downing, Jack Wright, Johnson Proctor, anyone besides himself. Yet the thought kept returning that he too might share the blame for the slaughter that had taken place that day, and he wondered what he would do when he got back on his feet. He wondered what he would counsel his friends and relatives to do.

And then another thought came into the already troubled mind of White Sut Beck. He could be, he realized, a fugitive in his own land. It was just possible, even probable, that the authorities in the Cherokee Nation would charge him with murder. It could even have already happened. He might have to remain in Arkansas to avoid arrest at home. Perhaps he would never be able to go home again.

12

Deputy Marshal Joseph Peavy finally made his way back to Fort Smith to report to Marshal Logan Roots in person. Deputy Charles Robinson was there already. Following a brief conversation with them, Roots took both men into the office of Commissioner Churchill.

"Now, tell me just exactly what happened out there, Peavy," Churchill said. "I mean on the first trial day when the killings occurred."

"Well, sir, me and Jake—Deputy Owens, I mean—we rode out to the trial along with the Becks and Jim Kesterson," Peavy said. "We had only just found out that the Cherokee chief had moved the trial from the courthouse to the Whitmire School. They said that he had done that because the schoolhouse could be defended easier. It only has one door and one window."

"Who said that?" the commissioner asked.

"Mr. Beck," Peavy replied. "White Sut Beck said that was the reason for it."

"The Cherokee authorities were anticipating a fight, then?" the commissioner asked. "You might even say, they were prepared for it?"

"Yes, sir, it seems thataway. Anyhow, when we got there we found the door guarded by Jack Wright, the Cherokee sheriff of Goingsnake District over there in the Nation, and a bunch of his Cherokee deputies. Well, I guess old White Sut Beck was afraid they weren't going to let him in. According to him, they was all friends of Proctor's, from the judge clear down to the guards at the door. Anyhow, he carried a shotgun to the door with him and made the sheriff step aside. Then he went on in.

"I was still out with the horses. Me and Jake, we wasn't supposed to do nothing but wait and see how the trial come out. So I didn't see exactly what happened in there, but I heard a shot. It was a shotgun blast. Then it sounded like everyone in there commenced to shooting. Pretty soon they was all outside and still shooting, and that's when Jake got hit.

"White Sut Beck come back to the horses shot twice clean through, and I decided to get him out of there, so I took him over to Cincinnati and got him a place to stay and some medical help. Then I got ahold of Charlie Robinson, Deputy Robinson here, and he said that he'd take care of contacting Marshal Roots here to find out what to do next."

"Who fired the shot that killed Deputy Owens?" the commissioner asked.

"I don't know that, sir, and I don't guess no one really knows, except maybe the one who done it, and I ain't real sure that even he would know. It seemed like everyone there was shooting back and forth. It was the worst gunfight I ever seen."

Commissioner Churchill took a few notes before looking up again. The others waited in silence.

"Thank you, Deputy Peavy," Churchill said. "Deputy Robinson, can you pick up the story from there?"

"Well, yes, sir, I believe I can," Robinson replied. "As soon as Mr. Peavy here contacted me, I went to the nearest telegraph and sent a wire to Marshal Roots. He wired me back to arrest those responsible. I got the names from Mr. Peavy and raised a posse. We rode across the line the very next morning and located the Whitmire School, the scene of the shootings, but by the time we arrived there, none of the participants were present.

"I was informed by Mrs. Whitmire, who lives just across the road from the school, that Mr. Proctor had gone home with an army of fifty armed Pin Indians around him. I was also able to discover that the trial had been conducted in short order that very morning, and that Mr. Proctor had been found not guilty. Apparently the new time and place of the trial had been kept secret. I went with my posse into Tahlequah and presented the chief with a request for his assistance in arresting the men in question."

"And what kind of response did you receive from Chief Downing?" Churchill asked.

"He refused to cooperate," Robinson said.

"Did he give you a reason?"

"He gave four reasons, sir. He said that my written request to him was not official. He said that our side had started the shooting and the Proctor side had shot back in self-defense. He said that we couldn't possibly know who had shot who out there, and he said that he did not believe that we had jurisdiction in the matter."

"Lewis Downing is a stubborn son of a bitch," Churchill said. "Mr. Robinson, do you have that list of names with you?"

"Yes, sir, I do," Robinson replied, reaching into his pocket to produce a folded piece of paper. "I kept a copy of the letter I submitted to Chief Downing. Here it is."

He handed the paper to Churchill, who smoothed it out carefully on his desk in front of him.

"Marshal Roots," he said, "I'm going to issue a federal warrant for the arrest of all of these men for murder, and I expect it to be served."

Outside on a bench at the edge of the courthouse yard under a large oak tree, sat four old Arkansas farmers. One of them produced a plug of tobacco and a penknife and passed them around. Each man cut himself a chaw and stuffed it into his mouth.

"What do you think about that Zeke Proctor business?" asked one old man.

"I knew old Zeke up at Shilo," said another. "He's a mean one. Always has been. He's killed about twenty men."

"You knew him?" said another.

"Yeah, I knew him. Well, I should say, I used to see him. He used to come into Shilo to get drunk, you know, because liquor's illegal over in the Nations. But he's a full-blood, long-haired Indian, and he don't speak a word of English, so I couldn't really get to know him, if you know what I mean."

"If he can't speak no English, how's he buy his liquor?"

"Oh, he knows money, all right, and besides, some of them liquor dealers up there are Indians themselves. He got it all right. And he's a mean drunk. Nice enough man when he's sober, but drunk—he'd kill you as soon as look at you. Gun, knife, or club, he don't care."

"Is that so?"

"That's right. Why, last week they say that four deputy marshals went into the Cherokee Nation and none of them come out. No one knows what become of them. I know. Zeke Proctor got them, all right. No one will ever see hide nor hair of them four again."

"Where'd you hear that?"

"Oh, I heard it around. I don't doubt the truth of it neither. Not a bit. There ain't nothing about ol' Zeke Proctor you could tell me that I wouldn't believe. The man ain't hardly human, I tell you. And mean? He's mean clean through."

"Twenty men?"

"Hell, yes. At least twenty."

Zeke Proctor rode with the two Walkingsticks to the home of Watt Christie. From there, Watt went with them to show them where Old Wolf lived. Tom Walkingstick had said that Old Wolf had the best medicine for avoiding capture and for winning fights.

"And he's my mother's father," Tom had said. "He'll help you."

Old Wolf's house was a one-room log cabin, and beside it was a small arbor. As the four riders approached the cabin, the door was pushed open from the inside and the old man stepped out. He stood there squinting for a moment, then recognized the riders.

"*'Siyo,*" he said. "Get down and come on over."

He spoke entirely in the Cherokee language, and he motioned toward his arbor. The visitors dismounted, secured their horses and walked to the arbor. Old Wolf shook hands with each of them in turn and motioned toward places to sit: a straight-backed chair, a tree stump, a split log that served as a bench. They all sat down, leaving the chair for Old Wolf. He took it.

"Old Wolf," Watt Christie said, "you know these two. They're your grandsons, I think."

"Yes. They don't come to see me often enough, but I can still remember them a little bit. That one's getting fat since the last time I saw him."

Tom ducked his head as everyone else had a good chuckle at his expense. Then Watt jerked a thumb toward Zeke.

"This is Zeke Proctor," he said. "He's come here for your help."

Old Wolf smiled widely and nodded.

"Zeke Proctor," he said. "Yes. I've heard about you. The white men in Arkansas say that you've killed a hundred men, and that you have a metal chest that can't be hurt by bullets. Maybe they think that you're Brass, the Gambler, come back to earth again."

They all chuckled at the old man's reference to the ancient Cherokee tale of Brass, a mythical character of Cherokee legend whose body was made of brass and who could change his shape at will.

"The lawmen from the United States are after Zeke, Grandfather," Tom Walkingstick said.

Robert J. Conley

"And the Beck family, Cherokees, they're after him too," John Walkingstick added. "We said that you could help."

"That's two different problems," the old man said, "but I think that I can help you out with both of them. It will take some time though. To do it right, these things take time."

The old man got up and found a large wooden bowl. He then produced some tobacco in a pouch and poured it into the bowl. For some time then he was engaged privately in mixing the tobacco with his hands and reciting something unintelligible in a low voice, occasionally putting something into the bowl with the tobacco.

At last he stopped and passed the bowl around. Each man there filled his own pipe from the bowl and smoked. Then Old Wolf went back to mixing and chanting. A second time he passed around the bowl. A second time they all smoked. This ritual was repeated four times, and at the conclusion of the fourth, the night was gone. The sun was beginning to show itself in the east over the tops of the tree-covered hills.

Old Wolf poured the tobacco mixture back into the pouch and handed it to Zeke.

"You know how to use this," he said. "Smoke it around your house. Smoke it in your house. Smoke yourself all over with it. Use it every day. Each day it will be stronger. It will keep harmful things away from you and away from your home."

"Wado," Zeke said.

"Now for the other," Old Wolf said. "You wait here. I'll be right back." He walked out from under the arbor and went into his house. In a moment he came out again, carrying in his hand a small notebook and a

108

stub of a pencil. He sat back down on his chair and glanced at Zeke.

"Do you read the writing?" he asked.

"Yes," Zeke said. "I can read."

"Good."

The old man thumbed through the notebook until he found what he wanted. Then, keeping his place with his thumb, he turned to the back of the notebook for a clean page and tore it out. Then he meticulously copied the words from the other page. He held the new copy out toward Zeke. Zeke took the paper and silently read what was written there in the symbols of the writing system given to the Cherokees by Sequoyah.

"You call on the Little Men," Old Wolf said, pointing with a finger straight up into the sky, "the Thunder Boys, you know. You call on them to help you. Read those words exactly, then spit on your hands. Rub it on your face. Rub it on your chest and belly. All over you. Do this four times, and the white man's bullets won't touch you."

Zeke put the paper in a coat pocket. *"Wado,"* he said.

By then Old Wolf had located another page in his notebook and was copying the words from that one. When he finished, he handed that sheet to Zeke. It was a short statement.

"If they come on you at once, by surprise," Old Wolf said, "say that to them. If you have to fight, you will win."

Zeke read the words silently.

You there in my path. I am as strong as you.

"There is one more," the old man said, and again he searched his notebook. Again he wrote. He handed the third sheet to Zeke. "This one you can say to keep them from finding you. They won't even come close when they look for you."

Zeke read again.

Your souls are lost, it said. *You are wandering about aimlessly. You don't know where you're going.*

Zeke put the third charm in his pocket, and he felt a surge of confidence sweep through his body. His own skills and physical powers were now reinforced by the mysterious powers Old Wolf was able to call down from on high.

Seeing that the business underneath the arbor was finished, the wife of Old Wolf came out of the house and invited everyone to breakfast. They ate and drank lots of coffee. John Walkingstick paid Old Wolf, and the visitors all mounted their horses to leave. Riding along with Watt Christie and the two Walkingsticks, leading Reb, Zeke Proctor felt like he had become the man who could not be killed.

— 13 —

Ellis Foreman was lying in his bed recuperating from the wound he had received during the gunfight at the Whitmire School. He had been a member of the jury and had not been armed. When the shooting had started, Ellis had jumped up out of his chair, thinking to run for cover, but a bullet had struck him in the back of his thigh. He had fallen to the floor and remained there bleeding until the fight came to an end a few minutes later. Then someone had helped him across the road to the Whitmire house, where Mrs. Whitmire had bound up his wound. Looking around himself at the other wounded and the dead, he thought at the time that he had been lucky. It could have been much worse.

Riders had gone out later to inform family members of the victims of the events that had taken place there, and finally Ellis's wife and her brother had come for him in a wagon. It had been a painful ride, but again he had something to be thankful for. His house was not far from the Whitmires'.

Because of his wound, Ellis had been relieved of jury duty. Judge Sixkiller had replaced him for the trial the next day. Ellis was thinking about getting up and trying to walk around. He had been in bed since the day of the fight, and he was getting bored. He also thought that it might be better for his leg if he gave it a little exercise. He was about to call out to his wife and tell her that, when he heard the sound of horses' hoofs arriving at his house.

"Who is it, Mavis?" he called out. "Who's coming?"

"I don't know," his wife yelled from the other room. "I'll go see."

The sounds of the horses were nearer. They seemed to be just outside, and Ellis could hear voices too. There's a bunch of them, he thought, whoever it is.

"Mavis?"

"There's about a dozen men out there," she said. "Maybe more. Maybe twenty. Stay where you are. I'll see who it is."

He heard her open the door and speak to the visitors, and he heard the response of one of the men.

"I'm Joe Peavy, ma'am. I'm a deputy United States marshal. These men with me are all sworn in. They're a duly constituted posse. I have here a warrant for the arrest of Ellis Foreman. Are you Mrs. Foreman?"

"I am. What do you mean you have a warrant for my husband? What for?"

"It's for the murder of Deputy Marshal Owens during the gunfight at the Whitmire School. Is your husband at home?"

"I'm in here," Ellis shouted. "Come in here and show me your warrant."

Mrs. Foreman hesitated a moment, then stepped aside. Joe Peavy walked cautiously into the house, slowly drawing his revolver out of its holster as he went. He wasn't about to get caught in another surprise gunfight. He gestured with his left hand for two of the possemen to follow him, and, drawing out their own revolvers, they did. Stepping into the next room, Peavy saw Foreman lying there in bed, covered with a worn, thin blanket.

"Are you Ellis Foreman?" he asked.

"That's my name. Who're you?"

"Joe Peavy, deputy United States marshal."

"What does the United States government want with me?" Foreman asked.

"You're wanted in connection with the murder of Deputy J. G. Owens at the Whitmire School," Peavy said. He glanced at one of his two backup men. "Pull back that cover," he said. "Watch out. He might have a gun under there."

"If I did," Foreman said, "you'd be dead already."

The posseman stepped up to the bed and pulled the cover off of Foreman with a jerk. Foreman was lying there in his long underwear, a bloodstained bandage on one thigh. Satisfied that Foreman had no weapons hidden under the cover, Peavy relaxed a little and put away his revolver.

"Mr. Foreman," he said, "you're under arrest. I'm going to have to ask you to get up and get your clothes on. You're going back to Fort Smith with me."

"I didn't kill anyone," Foreman said. "I didn't even have a gun on me, and I got shot anyway. See? Look at this. Shot through my leg for sitting on a jury. I'm all laid up here."

"We'll be careful of your leg, Mr. Foreman," Peavy said, "but you're going to have to go with us. I've got another little errand to run, but I'm going to leave these two men here with you to see that you get yourself ready to go by the time I get back. Oh, yeah." He reached into a vest pocket and pulled out a piece of paper which he handed to Foreman. "Here's your warrant. Now get ready."

From there, Peavy led the posse directly to the home of Arch Scraper. Scraper was in the yard when he saw them coming. He ran into the house and picked up a shotgun. Then he waited at the door, standing just inside, the gun pointed out. The posse pulled up close to the front porch, and Peavy held up a hand.

"No guns, boys," he said. "Not yet."

"What do you want here?" Scraper said.

"I'm Deputy U.S. Marshal Joe Peavy."

"I know who you are," Scraper replied. "What do you want?"

"I've got a warrant here for your arrest," Peavy said. "Now put down the gun and come on out, and there won't be no trouble."

"What does that warrant say?" Scraper asked. "I ain't broken no laws."

"It calls for your arrest along with some others for the murder of Deputy Marshal Owens."

"Hell," Scraper said, "I wasn't even armed when he got killed. I was sitting on the jury."

"You'll have to tell it to the judge," Peavy replied. "This here warrant calls for the arrest of every man who sat on that jury. You going to put down that gun?

You could kill me. Maybe one or two more, but the others would fill you full of holes."

Scraper hesitated, looking over the group in front of his house, obviously thinking it over, weighing the odds. He was outnumbered and way outgunned. He put the shotgun down inside the door and stepped out, holding his arms out at his sides.

"Hell," he said, "I guess I'll go along with you. If they've taken to hanging innocent men over at Fort Smith, well, so be it. A man goes when his time's up anyhow."

Peavy put handcuffs on Scraper's wrists and rode him double with one of the possemen back to the home of Ellis Foreman. There a wagon was waiting. Foreman had already been loaded into the back of the wagon, stretched out on a stack of quilts, his wounded leg propped up on a blanket roll one of the men had taken from behind his own saddle.

They made Scraper get down off the horse he had ridden and attached leg irons, then helped him up in the wagon bed beside Foreman.

"Huh," Foreman said to Scraper, "I see they got you too."

A posseman nodded toward Foreman as he spoke to Peavy.

"That one don't need no irons, Joe," he said. "Hell, he can barely walk with that hole in his leg."

"All right," Peavy said. "Let's get going. It's a long ride back to Fort Smith."

The two Walkingsticks were the first to see the group of armed men riding toward Zeke Proctor's house. They were lounging on the front porch of the house occupied by Elizabeth and the children. Tom

Walkingstick picked up a rifle and cranked a shell into the chamber. John stood up and drew his revolver out of its holster. He held it down at his side. The riders came closer.

"It's okay, John," Tom said. "They're some of our boys."

John put his six-shooter back into the holster and the two brothers stepped down off the porch to meet the riders. Cull and Frog were in the lead. Soldier, One, and Redbird Sixkiller were there. And there were others.

"'*Siyo,*" Tom said.

"'*Siyo,*" Frog said. "Where's Zeke?"

"He's out in the barn fussing over that gray horse," John replied. "What's up?"

"Peavy's running around in these parts with about twenty deputies," Cull said. "They've arrested Ellis Foreman and Arch Scraper. Taking them back to Fort Smith. The word is that they have warrants for Zeke, Judge Sixkiller, Isaac Vann, and a whole bunch more."

"I guess I'm even on that warrant," One Sixkiller said.

"And the whole jury," Frog added. "It looks like they want to arrest the whole Cherokee Nation except for the Becks."

Tom Walkingstick turned toward the barn and started walking. He spoke over his shoulder to the others.

"I'll fetch Zeke," he said.

In a short while he returned. Zeke, wearing his two Colt revolvers and carrying his Winchester rifle, was walking alongside him.

"Welcome, boys," he said. "Climb down and have some coffee. You hungry?"

"There's no time for that, Zeke," Cull said. "There's a federal posse out rounding up everyone they can get their hands on. They got Arch and Ellis, and they'll pretty likely be on their way over here. Your name's on their list. We came to get you out of here."

"Where are we going?" Zeke asked as Elizabeth stepped out onto the porch.

"Keetoowah meeting place," Cull replied. "In the hills south of here. You'll be safe there. There's others going after Judge Sixkiller and them to take them over there too. Those deputies won't even get close to any of you there. And if they do, we'll be ready for them."

"We got about fifty men," One Sixkiller said.

"I'll fix you a bedroll, Zeke," Elizabeth said. "You better go with them."

Zeke hesitated only a moment. "I'll get a few things out of the house," he said.

"I'll saddle your horse for you," John Walkingstick said.

"And old Reb," Zeke added. "Saddle him too."

White Sut Beck was sitting up in a stuffed chair in the corner of the bedroom of the home in Cincinnati where he had been a guest since the day of the shooting. He was drinking a cup of hot tea. Only recently had he regained enough strength to get out of bed and get dressed. He was moving about a little, but mostly he was sitting in the stuffed chair. It shouldn't be too much longer, he told himself, before he would be able to get around almost normally. Then after a little while, he'd be as good as new again. He was anxious to get back to his own home, to get back to work. He was tired of doing nothing but sitting and thinking, tired of wondering what would come next.

From his spot in the bedroom he heard the knock at the front door. He heard the door being opened and heard the voice of a man and the response of a woman. Then he heard the footsteps. The door to the bedroom was opened a bit from the outside, and the woman of the house peeked in.

"Sut," she said, "you have a visitor. Do you feel up to it?"

"Sure," he said. "Who is it?"

She opened the door wider and stepped aside, and Jim Kesterson stepped in. He held his hat in front of his belt buckle in both hands, and he grinned a sheepish grin.

"Howdy, Mr. Beck," he said. "I'm right glad to see you sitting up like that."

Beck frowned a little and set aside his teacup.

"Hello, Kesterson," he said. "What brings you here?"

"I just come to see how you're doing," Kesterson replied, "and to bring you some news."

"I'm doing all right," Beck said. "I'll be getting back home before long."

"Well, now," Kesterson said, "that's what I came to tell you. That's what the news is about. I didn't know whether you'd heard about it yet or not, so I thought I'd better come on over and tell you."

"Well, go on. What is it then?" Beck asked, not trying very hard to disguise the irritation in his voice.

"There's a warrant out for your arrest back over in

the Cherokee Nation. You go home, and they'll arrest you. For murder. For killing Johnson Proctor. They, uh, they hang you over there for that, don't they? Same as over here? You'd best stay over here in Arkansas where they got no authority. I thought you ought to know."

Beck's head dropped just a little, and he stared at the floor. He had anticipated the possibility of such a turn of events. Still, the news of its actual occurrence hit him hard. He was a Cherokee citizen. His home was in the Cherokee Nation. And now he could not go home. He would be a fugitive in his own land. He wondered if he would ever be able to go home again. Then he thought about Kesterson, the white man, going back and forth as he pleased, and that thought rankled more than any other just at that moment.

"Look at the bright side," Kesterson said with a grin. "The feds has got warrants for Zeke and the judge and the whole damn jury and a few others. Their warrants is good anywhere. Hell, that bunch ain't safe on either side of the line. At least you're safe over here. You got a place where you can rest easy."

"Kesterson," Beck said, "I suppose I should thank you for bringing me the news. Well, all right. Thank you. That's done. Now let me give you a little advice."

"Huh?"

"This whole mess is probably your fault, but I'm going to do you one last favor. I'm going to suggest that you leave this country. Go as far away from here as you can. Find someone to sponge off of besides Cherokee women."

"Now, wait a minute, Mr. Beck," Kesterson said. "I thought you and me was friends. That's the only

119

reason why I come by here to tell you what's happened. Why, I might have just saved you from getting yourself arrested. Maybe even hanged for murder."

"I realize that," Beck replied. "I'm returning the favor. I might be saving you from getting yourself shot and killed, if not by a Proctor, then maybe by a Beck. You never know."

"What have I ever done to you or any of yours?"

"Kesterson, you're no good. You're the worst kind of lazy, shiftless white trash. You've had your warning. Now get out of here."

Jim Kesterson left in a hurry, and White Sut Beck sat alone trying to remember what the whole fight had been about in the first place and wondering where it would all end.

— 14 —

They sat around a fire in a small clearing nestled in the thickly wooded Ozark foothills. It was late evening of a hot day, and a heavy fog hung in the humid air. All of the men gathered there were armed with at least one gun; most had two or three. Not everyone, though, sat in the clearing.

The only access to the clearing was a narrow pass that wound through the high, steep, rocky tree- and brush-covered hills. Here and there, at strategic points along the hillsides, armed men kept close watch on that pass. There would be no surprises at this gathering. No unexpected posses would come in waving their warrants.

Zeke Proctor sat near the fire. To his right was Judge Blackhaw Sixkiller. The Walkingstick brothers and the other men who had ridden with Zeke were either in the crowd around the fire or up along the hillside somewhere, part of the watch. Most of the men there

121

were full-blood Cherokees, and when they spoke, they spoke in the Cherokee language.

There was one they called their chief, and for the moment he sat in silence smoking a corncob pipe. He seemed to be deep in thought. Out of respect for that mood, the others were quiet too, all of them. At long last, the fire in his pipe bowl having died out, the chief tapped the dottle loose from the bowl into the palm of his hand, reached out and dropped it into the fire. Then he looked up at the solemn, anxious faces of the others around him.

"I think that we should hear from our friend, Blackhaw Sixkiller," he said. "He was there at the big fight. He was the judge at our brother's trial, and he's a member of our own Cherokee Nation council. He understands the ways of both governments, and he understands our Keetoowah ways. Let's hear from Blackhaw Sixkiller what he thinks."

There were murmurs of assent, and then there was silence again. Judge Sixkiller cleared his throat as he stood to speak.

"My friends," he said, "I'm going to try to explain the situation to you the way I understand it. It's a matter of what the white man calls 'jurisdiction.' That has to do with whose government has the authority where.

"This is our country. It's our nation. Our government has the authority here, and it has that authority from us, because we elect our government officials.

"We believe that we, through our elected officials, should have full authority in our own nation; however, the United States government has taken some of our authority, our jurisdiction, away from us. Every time we have made a treaty with the United States, we have lost either land or jurisdictional authority, usually both.

"One of the things, one of the areas of jurisdiction, the United States has taken away from us is the power to deal with people who are not citizens of our nation. Even when such persons commit crimes within our borders, the United States says that we do not have jurisdiction. They have it.

"This thing that has happened that has brought us all here together tonight in this place has developed into a jurisdictional dispute between the Cherokee Nation and the United States of America.

"As you all know, it started when our friend and brother, Zeke Proctor, sitting here by my side, went to confront James Kesterson, a white man, about a family matter. This Kesterson had married Zeke's little sister Elizabeth. That gave him rights as a Cherokee citizen, and he was making use of those rights, taking advantage of them. We think that brought him under our jurisdiction.

"Zeke and Kesterson got into an argument, and Kesterson went for a gun. He wasn't a very smart man. You all know that no man with any brains would pull a gun on Zeke Proctor."

Sixkiller paused for a chuckle that ran through the crowd following that last remark, and Zeke grinned and ducked his head, but he still puffed up a little.

"Well," the judge continued, "as usual, Zeke was faster with a gun than the other man. Unfortunately, this time, an innocent person got in the way. Polly Beck, Widow Hildebrand, was there, and she jumped in the way when Zeke shot at Kesterson, and she took the bullet that was meant for that white man, and she got killed."

Everyone present had heard the whole story by this time, yet they all sat quietly and patiently while the judge rehashed it. They knew that he was making legal and moralistic points with the tale, and they were all interested in hearing the way in which he would tell it.

"Kesterson got away. Zeke, because he's a law-abiding Cherokee citizen, gave himself up to the sheriff right away, and we had a trial scheduled in our own courts. That's the way it should be.

"But Kesterson kept on running until he got over to Fort Smith, and there he swore out a complaint against Zeke Proctor for shooting at him, a white man. He didn't say anything about his Cherokee wife. Nobody asked about his citizenship. The federal court issued the warrant for Zeke Proctor for assault on a white man.

"Now, my friends, the way I understand the law, I don't think that the United States ever had any business getting involved in this case. Kesterson had become a Cherokee citizen, and he had done it on purpose. He had done it for his own advantages. And he had done it by getting himself married to a Cherokee woman. Then, after that good Cherokee woman, Elizabeth Proctor—most of us know her, I think—had given that white man two little babies, he abandoned them, ran off and left them all alone, left her to do her best all by herself. Zeke went to get them and found them about starved, and he took them with him to his own home to care for.

"Any good Cherokee man would take up for his sister, and any good Cherokee man would look out for his sister's children. That's what Zeke was doing. It's unfortunate and it's sad that Polly Beck got in the way, but that's why Zeke gave himself up, because of what happened to her, and that's what the trial was for. Any way you look at it, I think, it was a Cherokee matter and not any business of the United States.

"But we know from long and bitter experience that the United States doesn't even pay very close attention to its own laws when it comes to dealing with the Cherokee Nation. We all know that the Supreme Court of the United States said that it was illegal for them to move us out here from our own ancient homelands in the east, and we all know how much good that did. Here we are."

Sixkiller again paused for effect and to allow his listeners to mutter agreement with his last statement and to express their own displeasure with the government of the United States. He waited for the murmurs to subside before he continued.

"Then we had another complication in this case. The trial date had been set, the place determined, and the judge selected, but the Beck family, that large family of mixed-blood Cherokees, went to Tahlequah to complain. They didn't like the judge. The judge was changed. Then the judge was changed again, and that's when I got appointed judge for the trial.

"Then the Becks allied themselves with Kesterson and with the United States government against their own Cherokee people and their own Cherokee government, and on the day of the trial, which was to be held at the Whitmire School—you all know where that is—they showed up heavily armed with a federal posse.

"Without giving any warning, and for no apparent reason, White Sut Beck stepped in the door and fired his shotgun. He killed Johnson Proctor right then. I saw it happen. Then another one came in and shot Moses Alberty. Moses was right beside me. I saw the whole thing.

"Nobody had a gun out pointed at White Sut Beck. Johnson and Moses didn't even have any guns on them. Those men stepped in the door and started shooting. Just like that. I was there. I saw it all.

"Well, after that, everyone seemed to start shooting on both sides. Men were killed on both sides. But one of the men killed on the other side was a white man and a deputy United States marshal.

"That's all the United States needed. That was their opening. But did they try to find out who killed their deputy? No. They didn't. Instead, they issued warrants for everyone who was there who wasn't with the Becks who they could find a name for.

"They have charged Zeke Proctor with the murder. They have charged me with the murder. They charged everyone who was sitting on that jury with the murder, and they've charged a few others with that same murder for good measure. I didn't think that lawman had that many bullet holes in him."

Again there were chuckles, and Sixkiller waited for them to pass.

"And I don't even think that it was a murder," he said. "I don't know who killed that white man, but whoever it was, he did it in self-defense. We were gathered there to conduct a legal trial in our Cherokee courts, and they came in and started shooting. What were we to do but defend ourselves?"

Sixkiller paused, and the murmurs this time were a

little louder, a little angrier than before, and this time he allowed them to go on a little longer.

"Well, we went ahead and had our trial the next day, and the jury determined that the death of poor Polly Beck was an accident," the judge continued.. "As far as the Cherokee Nation is concerned, and I have heard this straight from the mouth of our principal chief, as far as the Cherokee Nation is concerned, the matter is closed. That is, the matter of the killing of Polly Beck. That's what Chief Lewis Downing said.

"But now we have another matter before us, and that is the cold-blooded murders of Johnson Proctor and of Moses Alberty, and for those two acts, the Cherokee Nation has issued a warrant for the arrest of White Sut Beck. I understand that White Sut Beck is hiding out in Arkansas outside the boundaries of our jurisdiction. And as I said before, that should be the end of it, unless he ever tries to come home.

"But it isn't the end. The United States still insists on exercising its outstanding warrant for the arrest of any number of our people who are totally innocent, who were unarmed at the time of the fight, some of whom were injured, all of whom were victims rather than perpetrators. To show you the extent of the absurdity of their warrant, they even have listed on there for arrest, charged with murder, the name of Johnson Proctor, the unarmed man who fell dead as a result of the very first shot fired.

"And they have already acted on that warrant. Our good friends Ellis Foreman and Arch Scraper have already been arrested by a federal posse and taken to Fort Smith and jailed. Ellis Foreman was taken out of his sickbed where he was recuperating from a bad gunshot wound to his leg suffered in the very fight in question. He too was unarmed, yet he was shot, and he is accused of murder, and he has been jailed. Arch Scraper fortunately was not hurt in the shooting, but he too was unarmed, and he too has been accused and has been arrested and jailed.

"There is no logic on the side of the United States in this argument. There is no pursuit of justice involved. There is no reasonable defense for their actions. The only possible motive on the part of the United States of which I can conceive is that they are once again purely and simply attempting to steal away from us another area of jurisdiction, and they will try to do so at the expense of innocent lives."

Sixkiller sat down again. A long silence followed. It was obvious that the judge had finished with his remarks. At last, the Keetoowah chief stood to speak again.

"Judge," he said, "when these United States lawmen, these deputies, come in here to our country with their guns and with their paper—you called it a warrant, I think—to get Zeke and you and the others, do they have a right to do that, do you think?"

"In my opinion as a judge and as a member of the elected national council of our nation and as a Cherokee citizen," Sixkiller said, "I think that they have no right to attempt the arrest of any of the people named on that warrant. I see them as nothing more than foreign invaders. They have no more rights than would lawmen from Mexico or Canada or the Choctaw Nation."

The chief walked around the fire stroking his chin, looking over the entire crowd.

"What do you think?" he said. "All of you? If

anyone wants to say something, stand up and say it. Now's the time."

One man in the middle of the crowd stood up. "I'm not a smart man," he said. "Whatever you say and whatever the judge says, that's what I believe, and I'll do what you tell me I should do."

Another man stood. "Let's all stay right here," he said. "Those lawmen can't get anyone in here."

"If those lawmen come in here to try to arrest any Cherokees," said yet another, standing up to be seen, "let's kill them. That's all."

"Are there any other opinions?" the chief asked. "Does anyone else want to speak?"

He walked around the fire again, still looking out into the crowd as he moved, giving them all time to decide. No one else spoke out. No one stood to be recognized.

"Then we've decided," the chief said. "We are within our rights here. This is our land, and the lawmen from outside have no business here. Zeke Proctor, Judge Blackhaw Sixkiller, and all the others named on the white man's paper are our people. They're our citizens, our friends, our neighbors, our relatives. And we will protect them from all outsiders.

"And if any of our people, any of the Real People, any real Cherokees have to kill one or more of those white lawmen, we here will not consider him to be guilty of any murder. We'll consider him to be a Cherokee patriot protecting Cherokee citizens and Cherokee rights, and if anyone else finds out that he did that and should think him guilty of a murder, we'll protect him from those people too. That's our decision. Are we all agreed?"

Robert J. Conley

All heads in the crowd nodded affirmatively, and all voices responded in strong agreement. The Keetoowahs had, in effect, declared a defensive war on the United States of America.

"Good," the chief said. "Then that's our official position."

130

15

Clement Neeley Vann, former lieutenant colonel in Stand Watie's regiment of Confederate Cherokees, walked down the dimly lit hallway of the old boardinghouse in Washington, D.C., alongside Colonel William Penn Adair, Watie's flamboyant former chief of scouts. The two men moved along without speaking, looking at the numbers on the doors as they walked.

"Here it is," Adair said.

No one passing them by on the streets of the capital city would have taken the two men for American Indians. Alone, Vann might have been dismissed as a local businessman or government clerk. Adair, however, had the look of a frontier dandy, with his shoulder-length hair, mustache, goatee, and broad-brimmed hat. His appearance aside, Adair was a law school graduate.

They stopped at the door Adair had indicated, glanced at one another, and Adair rapped on the door. Vann reached into an inside coat pocket and pulled out a piece of paper. In a moment the door was opened by a tall, gaunt man with prematurely white hair and a full white beard. He was William Potter Ross, nephew of the late, longtime principal chief of the Cherokee Nation, John Ross. These three men made up the Cherokee Nation's delegation to the United States.

Of the three, Ross was the odd man, having served in the Indian Home Guard during the Civil War on the Union side of the cause. He was a Princeton graduate and a former editor of the Cherokee Nation's newspaper, *The Advocate.*

Ross hesitated for a moment, surprised by the visit. Even though the three men were, technically, colleagues, they were not the best of friends, having been on opposite sides of many battles in the past. He recovered his composure quickly, though, stepped aside while opening the door wide and, with a sweep of his long arm, invited the other two into his room.

"What's the purpose of this visit, gentlemen?" he asked.

"We have work to do at the capitol," Adair said. "Show him the letter, Clem."

Vann handed the letter to Ross, who read it through carefully.

"Oh, excuse me, gentlemen," Ross said. "Please sit down. We should probably discuss our strategy before we go charging the halls of Congress or the White House."

In the room was a table with four chairs, and Vann and Adair took seats there. Ross joined them and put the letter in the center of the table.

"If we were at home," he said, "we might have found ourselves on opposite sides of this dispute."

"Ross," Adair said, "if it was just a family feud between the Becks and the Proctors, I'd sure as hell side with the Becks. But that's not what it is. We all work for the Cherokee Nation, and the way I understand this business, it's a serious dispute between the Cherokee Nation and the United States over jurisdiction."

"That's certainly the way Chief Downing has explained it in this letter," Ross said. "I take it we're all together on this, then?"

"If we agree that we don't want to allow the United States to infringe on our sovereignty," Vann replied, "then we certainly are of a mind."

"The main points of the case seem to me to be as follows," Adair said. "The original trial of Ezekiel Proctor was a matter strictly Cherokee, as it involved the killing of a Cherokee citizen by another Cherokee citizen.

"There seems to have been some confusion over the matter of the attempted killing of James Kesterson because he's a white man, and he had a warrant sworn out against Proctor in the federal court at Fort Smith. However, he had married a Cherokee woman in order to secure for himself citizenship rights in the Cherokee Nation. So it's still a Cherokee case. The United States should never have been involved.

"In spite of that fact, a posse of federal lawmen showed up at the trial, seemingly including members of the Beck family. They started shooting, and the Cherokee deputies and others there at the trial shot back, killing, among others, a deputy U.S. marshal.

"Now the United States has issued warrants for the arrest of not only Proctor, but also the presiding judge at the trial and all of the jury. It's clear to me that the

United States is at fault here. It should never have been involved."

"And if the Fort Smith deputies are not called off soon," Vann added, "we could have a war on our hands."

"This could easily escalate into a major conflict," Ross said. "We have to do everything in our power to see that it does not. Where do we start, gentlemen?"

"I'd suggest," Adair said, "that we start with the Indian Bureau. From there we'll go to the members of Congress."

"Those we can reach," Ross added.

"Yes," Adair said. "They're certainly not all approachable, especially by Indians. Then, if we don't get satisfaction from either of those routes, we'll go directly to President Grant." He stood up. "Agreed?"

Vann stood as well. "I agree," he said.

Ross stood and extended his hand across the table toward Adair. Adair took it in his and gripped it hard.

"Agreed," Ross said. He then shook hands with Vann. "Shall we go, then?"

"Yes," Adair said. "Let's go. We've got a lot of talking to do."

Joe Peavy was back in the Cherokee Nation again. Again he had a posse of twenty men. Some were the same men as before. Most were new recruits. They rode to the home of Jane Harlan, and as they approached, the three children playing in front of the house ran into the woods nearby. Jane stepped out on the porch, drying her hands with a dishrag. She frowned as the riders came up to within a few feet of where she stood.

"Is this the home of Zeke Proctor?" Peavy asked.

"Zeke don't live here," Jane replied. "He visits sometimes. Sometimes he stays three or four days."

"I was told that this is his home," Peavy said.

"Zeke runs three farms, mister," Jane said. "Who are you anyway?"

"I'm a deputy United States marshal. Joe Peavy's my name, and I've got a warrant for the arrest of Zeke Proctor."

"From what I hear, you've got a warrant for the arrest of just about everyone except White Sut Beck. Is my name on your warrant?"

"No, ma'am," Peavy replied. "I was told that you are the common law wife of Zeke Proctor and the mother of one of his children."

"I guess you could say that. White men always call Indian marriages common law."

"Then this is his home?"

"It's one of them. Like I told you, he don't live here. He just visits now and then."

"Is he in the house now?"

"You mean right now?"

"Yes, ma'am. That's what I asked you. Is he in the house right now?"

"No. He ain't."

"Well, I'm going to have to take a look for myself," Peavy said as he swung down out of the saddle.

"I guess I can't stop you," Jane replied.

"No, ma'am," Peavy said, slowly taking his revolver out of its holster. "You can't." He turned and gestured toward one of his possemen. "You come with me," he said, and he pointed at two others. "You two go out and check the barn. Be careful. The rest of you keep your eyes open."

The three designated possemen took out their

weapons. Two of them headed for the barn, still mounted. The third dismounted and followed Peavy into the house. Jane stayed on the porch, frowning at the possemen who remained in front of her, sitting on their horses. Peavy and his companion returned in a short time. The house was not very big, and a thorough search did not take long.

"Well," Peavy said, "he ain't in there."

"I told you," Jane said. "You ain't going to ride up on Zeke that easy."

"Where is he, Mrs. Proctor?" Peavy asked.

"I don't know," Jane said. "He rode out of here when he heard about your warrant. Right after you arrested them other two."

"Foreman and Scraper?"

"That's right."

"Where did he go?"

"I don't know. He didn't say. But I wouldn't tell you if I did know."

"Then how the hell do I know if you're telling me the truth now?" Peavy asked.

"I guess you don't," Jane said.

The other two possemen came riding back from the barn. The nearest one called out to Peavy as he drew near.

"There ain't nobody out there," he said. "There ain't even no riding horses. Just an old harness team. That's all."

Joe Peavy climbed back up into his saddle. He gave Jane a hard look.

"The next time you see your husband, Mrs. Proctor," he said, "you tell him that things'll go a lot better for him if he turns himself in."

"If he turns himself in, you'll hang him," Jane said.

"He'll get a fair trial."

"In Fort Smith? In the federal court? Ha."

Peavy turned his horse and spurred it without another word, and his posse followed him down the lane and away from the house. From the woods three pairs of eyes watched. When the posse disappeared from view, the children came back out to play.

At Zeke's other home, Peavy and his posse found Elizabeth and the children sitting at their table eating a meal. Peavy barged in accompanied by two possemen. The others were outside waiting. Elizabeth jumped up from the table. The children sat still, frightened.

"It's all right," Peavy said. "I'm Deputy United States Marshal Joe Peavy. I've got a warrant for the arrest of Zeke Proctor, and I'm here looking for him."

"Well, he's not here," Elizabeth said, "so get out of here. You're scaring the kids."

"They don't need to be scared," Peavy replied. "No one's going to do nothing to them or to you. We're just looking for Zeke Proctor."

"Well, I just told you he's not here."

"Are you Mrs. Proctor?"

"I'm Zeke's sister. I'm Mrs. Kesterson."

"Oh," Peavy said, "I see. Well, we're just going to check the other rooms before we leave, Mrs. Kesterson."

"I wish you white men would leave Zeke alone," Elizabeth said. "He hasn't done anything for you to be hounding him like this."

Peavy had gone into a bedroom. He came back out and glanced at Elizabeth.

137

"He killed a woman," Peavy said.

"He was tried for that and acquitted."

"And he killed a deputy marshal. A friend of mine. Jake Owens."

"I heard all about that gunfight," Elizabeth said. "Your side started shooting first, and no one knows who shot that deputy."

"The courts will straighten it all out," Peavy said. "That's why Zeke Proctor ought to give himself up. If he's not guilty, it'll come out in court. You tell your brother that when you see him again."

The other man came back into the room. "There's no one else in the house, Joe," he said.

Peavy looked at Elizabeth. "I don't suppose you'd tell me where I can find him," he said.

"I wouldn't tell you if I could."

Peavy sighed. He was getting the same answer from everyone he questioned about Zeke Proctor, Cornick Sixkiller, and all the others. It was becoming clear that the federal marshals would get no cooperation from either the Cherokee citizens or the government of the Cherokee Nation in this matter. He was glad he had twenty men with him. He was beginning to feel very conspicuous and very vulnerable in the Cherokee country.

"We're going to check out the barn before we leave, Mrs. Kesterson," he said.

"You won't find anything," Elizabeth replied.

"Well," Peavy said, "I probably believe you, but I guess I just have to check it out for myself anyway. We'll ride on as soon as I take a look in there."

Elizabeth stood at the door and watched as Peavy and his posse rode over to the barn. She saw Peavy wave an arm, and then three men rode inside. They came back in a moment, and the whole posse rode away. She watched until she could no longer see them. Then she shut the door and latched it.

"Go on and eat, children," she said. "They're gone now. Everything's all right."

— 16 —

Riley Maw waited in the thick underbrush of the woods that grew beside the road that ran from Cincinnati to Shilo where it intersected with the road from Shilo into the Cherokee Nation. It was still dark, but soon it would be dusk. Maw had slipped away from the Keetoowah camp earlier in the heavy darkness. Maybe the white men couldn't get into the Keetoowah camp without being seen, but a Cherokee could get out.

He waited patiently, but there was fear in his heart. He had been careful, but it was always possible that he had been seen or that he would be missed. He knew what he would say, though, if anyone should confront him with his absence. He had missed his wife, and he had gone to see her. That was all.

There were no real commands in the Keetoowah camp. The men who were there were strictly volunteers. The Cherokees did not really know such a thing as absolute authority over their lives. Even during the war, the officers, especially the white officers, had complained that the Cherokee soldiers would go home if they took a notion to do so. Perhaps they missed their families, or they thought that there was work to be done at home. Maybe they got tired of riding or walking around looking for other soldiers to fight. Still, Maw felt some fear.

Then he heard something in the distance. The sky was gray, no longer black, so it was about time. He listened hard, and the sound became clearer, then identifiable. It was one horse, shod. One rider approaching at an easy pace. He waited and he watched.

When he first saw the horse and rider, they made a silhouette in the middle of the road. He stayed hidden, and he waited. It could be anyone. The rider came slowly. He was looking around as if he were watching for something—or someone. When he reached the intersection, he stopped. Then Maw recognized the deputy marshal, and he stepped out of the brush.

The deputy flinched a little from Maw's surprise appearance.

"It's me," Maw said. "Come over to the side of the road."

The deputy moved over close to where Maw stood, still close to the safety of the brush.

"Do you have the information I want?" he said.

"I've been with them," Maw replied.

"Zeke Proctor?"

"He's there. Judge Sixkiller too, and most of the others. They're saying this is war. They'll fight you."

"How many armed men are there?"

"At least fifty."

141

"Will you lead us to them?"

"No. I can tell you how to get there. I can even draw you a map. But to get to the camp, you have to go through a narrow pass. There are guards up on the hillsides watching all the time. They'll know you're coming. I don't think that you can get in there. It would be better to wait for Zeke and the others to come out."

"That won't be up to me," the deputy said. "Tell me where this camp is located. I'll report it back to the marshal in Fort Smith. He'll make the decision about what to do."

At the Keetoowah camp Zeke Proctor sat staring into the fire. He wondered what his children were doing, and he thought about them one by one: Zeke Jr., Charlotte, Francis, the triplets, Linnie, Minnie, and Willie. He longed to hold them each in his arms and kiss them. He wondered if he ever would again.

And he thought of Jane and of the pleasures of being in her bed. And then he thought with a deep sadness of Rebecca. He would miss Rebecca as long as he lived. He knew that. But untimely death had been commonplace throughout the life of Zeke Proctor. He had grown up with it, and he had grown used to it.

He had been old enough, at seven, for the vivid memories of the Trail of Tears to stay with him, and he had seen people die all along the way: men and women, old and young. And after the removal, after they had settled in their new homes, the factional killings had begun. He had seen some of that violence. Family friends and relatives had been killed.

Then the white man's Civil War had come along,

and the Cherokees had allowed themselves to be drawn into that. Zeke had killed, and he had seen his friends die in battle. Yes, untimely death had been all too common throughout the life of Zeke Proctor. What's wrong with a world, he wondered, where a man grows used to such things?

He knew what the old-timers would say. The Cherokees had too readily accepted things from the white man's world. It had started with steel knives and pots, glass beads and cloth, things that had made life easier. Then there were guns, blankets, and livestock. Cattle and hogs and horses all had been brought to the Cherokees by the white men.

The Cherokees' acceptance of these things into their world had upset the precarious balance that had existed between the upper and lower worlds, thus unleashing into this world a general chaos. Perhaps that was all true. Zeke didn't know.

But he tried to imagine a world without horses and cattle and hogs, without his guns, without the steel tools he used so much, and he could not. Even if he could have done so, he did not want to go back to what the world had been like before the arrival of the white man. He even thought with a silent chuckle that he would not exist had it not been for the arrival of the white man, for his own father was a white man. He wondered if he should feel guilty for having such thoughts.

Zeke was relieved to have his thoughts interrupted by the approach of Tom Walkingstick. He motioned to the split log bench on which he sat. "Pull up a chair, Tom," he said.

Walkingstick sat down and took a pipe out of his

pocket. Zeke pulled out his own tobacco pouch and handed it to Walkingstick.

"Wado," Walkingstick said.

He started filling his pipe from Zeke's pouch while Zeke dug into another pocket for his own corncob pipe. Walkingstick handed the pouch back to Zeke, then stood up to walk to a nearby small campfire for a flame. When he returned to the bench with a small burning stick, Zeke had filled his own pipe. The two men lit their tobacco from the stick. For a few moments they sat and smoked in silence. Then Walkingstick spoke again.

"Riley Maw has disappeared," he said.

"There's a lot of people here," Zeke said. "Some out there on the side of the hill. He could be anywhere."

Walkingstick shook his head. "He's not here," he said. "There's been men out looking for him."

"Well," Zeke said, "maybe he got tired of hanging around here and went home. I don't want nobody hanging around here because of me if he don't really want to be here."

"Do you know Riley very well?"

"I've seen him around."

"You know his wife?"

"No."

"She's a Bryant."

"Bryant?" Zeke said.

"They're related to the Becks."

"Oh," Zeke said. "I see. Related to the Becks, huh? Old Riley Maw. Can't find him anywhere, huh? He was here yesterday. I seen him, all right."

"He's gone now," Walkingstick said.

"Didn't say anything to anybody about where he was going?"

"Not a word," Walkingstick said.

"Not a word, huh?" Zeke repeated. "Just slipped off in the night."

Marshal Logan Roots sat in front of the desk of James H. Huckelberry, United States District Attorney for the Western District of Arkansas, with authority, from the United States, over all of Indian Territory. Huckelberry had on his desk a file on the Zeke Proctor case. He was obviously irritated.

"Why haven't we been able to bring these men in, Logan?" he asked.

"Mr. Huckelberry," Roots replied, his own frustration showing in the lines on his face and in his strained voice, "we arrested two of them, and they've made bond. They were released and ordered to show up in court in the November session."

"What about the others, especially Ezekiel Proctor?"

"They're hid out in the hills with an army of Indians to protect them," Roots said. "My information is that there's at least fifty well-armed men in a valley that's accessible only through one narrow pass. We had an informant in the camp, and he advised us that the best thing for us to do was to wait for Proctor and the others to come out."

"That could be a long wait," Huckelberry said, "and I for one do not believe that we can afford to wait. Every day we allow these Cherokees to defy the authority of the United States government, this court loses respect."

"We're not getting any help from the Cherokee Nation either," Roots said. "Usually they cooperate with us in tracking down and arresting outlaws over there, but not in this case."

"It seems that it's worse than that," Huckelberry said. "I have here a letter from one of your own deputies, James Donnelly, that states that the government of the Cherokee Nation is actually in league with Proctor and the Pin Indians. He claims that Chief Downing used his influence to get Proctor acquitted in the Cherokee courts. He says that Proctor and his gang actually laid an ambush at the Whitmire School for Deputies Peavy and Owens and their posse. He says that the Pins have sworn to kill every Indian or citizen of the Cherokee Nation who dares to give testimony or information on any other Indian or citizen of the Cherokee Nation in United States courts."

Roots felt his face burn a little. It rankled him that one of his deputies had gone over his head and complained to Huckelberry. It was a challenge to his own rank and authority, and he thought that he'd have a word or two with Donnelly as soon as it was convenient.

"Well, sir," he said, "I don't know about all that. I do know that we're getting no help out of them."

"It seems to me," Huckelberry said, "that the Cherokee Nation is dangerously close to being in open rebellion against the United States, and we don't seem to be able to handle the situation here with our resources. I'm going to write a letter to the attorney general in Washington, D.C., asking for his help in our attempt to administer the decision of the court. I'm going to request that he send troops up here from Fort

Sill to attack this Pin Indian camp and bring in Zeke Proctor and his gang."

Riley Maw was riding slowly back toward the Keetoowah camp. He was timing his ride so that he would not arrive until after dark. He had gotten out undetected. He figured that he could get back in just as easily. He had thought about staying home, but decided against that. The others might grow suspicious of him if he stayed away. But if he returned, he would likely find that they had not even missed him. He might even be able to gather more information.

Zeke Proctor or Judge Sixkiller or some of the others might decide to go somewhere, and if he were back in the camp, he would know about that. Then he could tell the U.S. deputies or even White Sut Beck. And so he was going back, but he was going slowly. He did not want to arrive too early. He would need the cover of darkness.

He rounded a bend in the road, and there, waiting, standing in a line across the road, were four Cherokee men, each holding a rifle in his hands. He recognized them all from the camp. Startled, he pulled back the reins and stopped his horse. He tried to regain his composure and act as if nothing was wrong.

"Hello, boys," he said, but he spoke in Cherokee. "You surprised me here."

The four men stood mute, and Maw smiled a broad, nervous smile.

"What is this?" he asked. "Is something wrong?"

Still they made no response.

"I went home for a little visit, you know? I'm on my way back now. I wasn't gone very long."

The man on the far right cranked a shell into the

147

chamber of his rifle, and the other three followed his example. Maw flinched at the ominous sound, and his horse stamped nervously and snorted.

"What are you doing?" Maw said as he watched the men raise the rifles to their shoulders. He clawed desperately for the revolver stuck in his belt, but before he could even grip its handle, a rifle bullet smashed into his chest. He jerked backward in the saddle. A second bullet ripped through his stomach, and he slumped forward. A third bullet tore his shoulder, and a fourth took off a piece of his skull. His body went limp, and slowly it slipped out of the saddle and fell into the road. The riderless animal snorted, stamped around, turned, and ran back down the road toward its home.

— 17 —

Marshal Logan Roots was still seething inside from the implication made by District Attorney Huckelberry that he couldn't do his job without the aid of the United States Army. He knew that Huckelberry was going to request that troops be sent into the Cherokee Nation, but he also knew that it would take time for the government to respond to the request. He could act faster than that. Back in his own office, he had word sent to Deputy Donnelly. Soon Donnelly was seated in the marshal's office.

"Jim," Roots said, "Huckelberry's asking the government to send troops in to take care of this Zeke Proctor deal." He leaned back in his chair and studied Donnelly's face for any reaction. He could see none. Donnelly made no reply.

"You know what that means, don't you?" Donnelly shrugged. "It means that he does not think that we are capable of doing our jobs. We can't keep a handle on things here. It means that he thinks I'm incompetent, and he thinks you're incompetent. Do you like having someone think that you're incompetent?"

"No, sir, I don't," Donnelly replied. "Not particularly."

"Well, I don't either. Not particularly or any other way. I don't like it a damn bit. Now, do you know what we're going to do about it?"

"No, I don't. Not until you tell me."

"You are going over there to get Zeke Proctor."

"I am?"

"Yes. I selected you most especially," Roots said, "because I know that you are particularly concerned about this case. Aren't you?"

"Well, yes, I am."

"You are so concerned about this case that you have written a letter direct to Mr. Huckelberry, haven't you?"

Donnelly ducked his head and fiddled with his hat brim in his lap. "Uh, yes, I did. I told him what I thought about the way the Cherokee Nation is treating us on this deal. That's all."

"That's all right, Jim," Roots said, but there was an edge to his voice that kept Donnelly from believing what he had just said. "That's the reason I called you in. I don't want to put just anybody in charge of this operation. I want a man who is genuinely concerned, who is concerned enough to have put his opinion in writing and sent it right over the top of his supervisor's head straight to the district attorney of the whole district of Western Arkansas. That's the kind of man I want in charge of this operation."

"Yes, sir," Donnelly said.

"Now you draw all the supplies you need," Roots

said, "and you ride over to Cincinnati and look up Joe Peavy. Then the two of you go on to Shilo and find Charlie Robinson. The three of you raise yourselves up a posse, however many men you think you need. Peavy and Robinson know where Zeke Proctor and the others are hiding out. They've had information from an informant. Go in there and arrest Zeke Proctor and all the others you can find whose names are on that warrant. Bring them back for trial if you can. If they resist arrest, do what's necessary, but bring them back one way or the other. Do you understand me?"

"Yes, sir," Donnelly said, rising up from the chair, relieved that the interview seemed to be over. "Yes, sir, I believe I do."

There were twenty-seven of them altogether, with Jim Donnelly in the lead. They were following the directions given to Joe Peavy by the late Riley Maw. The men were all heavily armed, and most of them seemed to be anxious for a fight. Some of them were mixed-blood Cherokees, relatives of White Sut Beck. Several others, mixed-blood and white, were former Confederate soldiers or southern sympathizers. All of them, for one reason or another, were strongly opposed to Zeke Proctor and the faction of Cherokees associated with him.

It was late evening when they arrived at the pass that would lead into the Keetoowah camp. Donnelly raised a hand to bring the posse to a halt. He waited a moment for the dust from the horses' hoofs to settle. Then he nodded in the direction of the pass. "That the way?" he asked.

151

"I'd bet on it," Peavy said. "From the directions Maw give me, I'd say that's the place right there."

"So we've got to ride through the pass to get to the camp?" Donnelly asked.

"That's the way I understood it," Peavy replied. "Right through it."

"Let's all dismount and settle down here for a few minutes," Donnelly said. "Rest the horses and ourselves. Talk about strategy. Check our weapons."

The posse dismounted and lounged at the side of the road. Donnelly, Peavy, and Robinson sat down on the ground together. Some of the men gathered around to look over their shoulders and listen. Others stretched themselves out on the ground, apparently thinking that, if there was anything they needed to know, they would be told.

"Fellows," Donnelly said, "I wonder if we took the time to scout around a bit could we find another way into that camp?"

"According to Riley Maw," Peavy replied, "there's no other way. That's it."

"Hell," Donnelly said, "there's got to be another way in."

Robinson swept his arm toward the hills that surrounded them. "Take a look," he said. "The hills are too steep, and the underbrush is too thick. Even if we could find a way, it'd take us a week to cut our way through. And they'd hear us coming long before we could see them."

"You don't even think there'd be any sense in trying?" Donnelly asked, a bit of a whine in voice.

"I can't see no reason for it," Peavy replied.

"Waste of time," Robinson said.

"It sure would be nice if we could find a way to kind of sneak in on them," Donnelly said wishfully.

"I don't think there is any sneaking on this case," Peavy said. "It's a goddamned head-on raid or nothing."

"Well, all right," Donnelly said, standing up with a loud grunt. He stepped out into the road and faced his posse. At least half of the men were not paying any attention to them, so he raised his voice to a moderate yell. "Hey there, boys. Can I have y'all's attention here for just a minute? Come on. Pay attention here."

The small conversations stopped, and all of the posse turned their eyes toward Donnelly. He cleared his throat loudly and hitched his pants up, leaving his thumbs hooked in his waistband.

"Boys," he said, "I need a couple of volunteers for a little job of scouting."

He waited for a very quiet moment while men looked at one another. At last a hulking blond stood up.

"Hell, I'll go," he said.

The man who had been sitting next to him, a small, wiry man, then sprang to his feet. He spoke, not to Donnelly, but to the blond.

"I'll go with you, Billy Bob," he said.

"Come on over here, boys," Donnelly said, motioning the two volunteers to follow him back to his plotting place beside the road. He squatted down, looking toward the entry to the pass. "You see that over there?" he said. "That little opening over there? It leads into a pass that goes on down into a valley. That valley's where Zeke Proctor is supposed to be hiding out. Now, I don't want to go charging in there

153

with all these men. We'd make so damn much noise that anybody down there would get all the warning he'd need. He'd be long gone before we could get close. You see?"

"Yeah," Billy Bob said.

"Well, that's what I want you for," Donnelly said. "I want you two to ride on down into that pass real slow and easylike. Scout it out. Find that valley and look it over. Then come back here, still keeping quiet, and tell us what you found, so we'll know how to go into it. All right?"

"Sure," Billy Bob said. "We'll spy it out for you. Come on, Homer."

Homer and Billy Bob headed for their horses. When they rode by Donnelly on their way into the pass, Donnelly called out to them, "Be careful now. We'll stay right here till you get back."

The two volunteer scouts made no response other than a wave of their arms as they rode into the entrance to the pass. It was narrow and rocky, but a clear path was visible.

"Somebody's been using this," Homer said.

"Yeah," Billy Bob said. "Quite a bit, I'd say."

They rode on in silence for a while under a canopy of large old oak trees. Only a step or two away from the path, the woods appeared to be almost impenetrable with a thick undergrowth of blackberry and huckleberry bushes. Overhead a gray squirrel scolded, and a bluejay screeched out his annoyance at their trespass.

Then the pass widened a little. The hillsides still rose sharply on either side of the riders, but the tree branches no longer formed a roof over their heads. The tangle of underbrush was farther away. The path was wide enough so that Homer, who had been taking up the rear, pulled up to ride alongside Billy Bob.

"You see anything yet?" he asked.

"No, I ain't," Billy Bob replied, "but I don't like it."

He stopped his horse, and Homer did the same. Billy Bob was studying the hillsides.

"What is it, Billy Bob?" Homer asked.

"I don't know. Maybe nothing. Let's go on, but keep your eyeballs peeled."

He urged his mount ahead slowly, easily, looking up and down the hillsides to the right and the left. Homer moved alongside him still, but a little behind. His movements were becoming quicker, jerky, nervous. Then he almost fell out of his saddle, startled by a voice that seemed to come down out of the clouds. It was clear and resonant, and seemed to soar right over their heads.

"Go back," it said.

The two riders stopped again. Billy Bob pulled the Winchester rifle out of its scabbard and cranked a shell into the chamber. He looked around in desperation for a body to go with the voice he had heard, but in vain. He could see nothing but the thick woods on the hillsides. It was as if there had been no voice, as if he had imagined it. Homer eased out his own rifle, looking to Billy Bob for direction.

"Get down," Billy Bob said, and he swung easily down out of the saddle. Homer climbed down too. "Come on," Billy Bob said, and, leading his mount by the reins, he started forward slowly on foot.

"Turn around and go back."

The voice sounded again. Again the two scouts stopped in their tracks. Again they looked. Again they saw nothing.

"Billy Bob?" Homer said.

"Come on," Billy Bob replied. "Hell, we got a job to do."

He had taken only three steps when the rifle sounded, and an instant later dust was kicked up just a few feet in front of him.

"Take cover," Billy Bob shouted, and he ran for the side of the path, throwing himself onto the ground behind some rocks there. Homer ran to the opposite side of the pass and jumped into a tangle of blackberry bushes.

"Ow," he cried. "Goddamn. Ow. Damn stickery thorns."

Another shot rang out, and the two horses, abandoned in the path, nickered and spun around in circles. Then one ran back in the direction from which they had come. The other ran forward.

"Billy Bob," Homer said in a loud whisper. "The horses!"

"Shut up," Billy Bob said. "Watch that hillside."

"Which one?"

"Just watch."

Another shot hit the rocks in front of Billy Bob, and he snuggled down into the earth as much as he could. Then the voice sounded once again.

"Go back," it said.

"Homer," Billy Bob said. "They're giving us another chance. Let's take it."

"We ain't got no horses," Homer whined.

"You got two feet," Billy Bob said. "Use them."

He stood up and ran back toward the road, and Homer tore himself loose from the bushes to run after him.

156

"Ow," he shouted. "Ow. I'm bleeding all over like a stuck pig. Wait for me, damn it! Wait for me."

Donnelly and the others heard the shots. A few minutes later one horse came running back out onto the road. They were trying to decide what to do next.

"We can't leave them in there," Peavy said. "We got to go in after them."

"We don't want to run into whatever they run into, though," Donnelly replied. "We got to have a plan."

"That's what they went in ahead of us for," Robinson said. "What's your plan?"

"We're wasting time," Peavy said. "Let's get mounted and go on in there. Come on."

Peavy ran for the horses and jumped into his saddle. He had turned the horse and was heading for the opening into the pass when Billy Bob came running out onto the road. Peavy hesitated a moment. Homer came out behind Billy Bob. Both men were running and panting heavily. Peavy dismounted again and walked back over to where Donnelly and Robinson waited. The two scouts trotted over to join them.

"Well," Donnelly said, "what happened?"

"Let them catch their breath," Peavy said.

"They're down there in that pass," Billy Bob said between heavy breaths. "We never even got close to the valley."

"Did you see them?" Donnelly asked.

"Never seen a one," Billy Bob replied. "They yelled and shot. That's all. They could pick us off easy down there one at a time."

"I'm bleeding like a stuck pig," Homer said.

"Did you get hit?" Peavy asked.

"No," Homer said. "I hid in a goddamned blackberry bush, and it was full of thorns. Real stickery thorns. That was the most thorniest blackberry bush I ever seen."

"Well, Jim?" Peavy said.

"It'd be suicide to go in there," Billy Bob said.

"Aw, hell," Donnelly said, "let's go back. I'll report to Marshal Roots what we run into here."

So without having seen a single one of their prey, the super posse from Arkansas mounted up, turned around, and headed for home. Donnelly's biggest worry, though, was how he was going to face the wrath of Marshal Roots.

18

H. R. Clum, Acting Commissioner of Indian Affairs, sat waiting to be ushered into the office of Ulysses S. Grant, President of the United States. He was a little nervous and apprehensive. It was not every day that he was called upon by the president. He was pleasantly surprised, and put at his ease, when the president himself, and not some underling, opened the door and looked out at him.

"Clum," President Grant said, "come on in here."

He was brusque, but not rude. It was Grant's manner. Clum noticed right away, for example, that Grant had actually smiled at him. Clum stood up quickly and walked into the office. Grant closed the door behind them and walked around to sit behind his massive desk. He was puffing a cigar, and the smoke was, as always, annoying to Clum. He did his best to pretend not to notice.

"Sit down," Grant said, and Clum sat in a large

plush chair directly across the desk from Grant. "I guess you know why I called you in here."

"I believe it was something to do with the case in the Cherokee Nation," Clum replied.

"Yes. From what I hear, the Cherokee Nation is on the verge of war with the United States. Hell, that's the last thing anybody would expect from the Cherokees. The last several wars they've been involved in, they've been in our goddamned army."

"Yes, sir."

"I'm hearing from the attorney general that he has gotten correspondence from the district court at Fort Smith, Arkansas, that there is actually a need for federal troops in the area. This man Proctor, they say, murdered an Indian woman and shot at a white man, and the Cherokee courts, under pressure from their own chief, turned him loose.

"Then they say, Proctor and his gang killed a deputy United States marshal and several members of his posse. They are now hiding out in the hills with a small army, well-equipped with guns and ammunition, and well-fortified. The United States court has appealed to the Cherokee authorities for assistance in this matter and have met with refusal. They have even suggested that the government of the Cherokees is assisting the fugitives."

Grant paused a moment while he rolled some dead ashes off the end of cigar into a large brass tray beside him.

"Mr. President," Clum said.

"Wait a minute," Grant said. "That's the story I'm getting from Fort Smith. I've also heard from the Cherokee delegation here in Washington. They've had communication from Chief Downing, and they're telling a completely different tale.

"They say that the posse in question wrongly interfered in a Cherokee matter, and, in fact, actually started the shooting. Then, they say, the court at Fort Smith issued a number of warrants for murder on people who were not even participants in the fight. Some of these people who are now being hounded by the federal authorities, they say, were in fact unarmed, innocent bystanders who were wounded by the gunfire."

"Yes, sir, I've heard that story too," Clum said.

"The situation down there now, as I understand it," the president said, "is this: the United States court has warrants for the arrest of Zeke Proctor and a number of others for the murder of Deputy Owens. The fugitives are resisting arrest most successfully.

"At the same time, the Cherokee Nation has a warrant for the arrest of a man called White Sut Beck, who, they say, was a member of the posse and was the one who actually fired the first shot that began the battle.

"They have a Mexican standoff down there, and the D.A., Huckelberry, wants the army brought in. Now, have I left anything out?"

"No, sir," Clum replied. "I don't believe so. I think that you've accurately defined the situation and the two opposing points of view."

"Clum," Grant said, "I don't know who's telling the truth and who's lying to me, and I'm damned if I'm going to send the United States Army into the Cherokee Nation when I don't know what the hell I'm sending them for. I want you to get to the bottom of this. I want an investigation, a report, and a recommendation, and I want it before somebody starts a goddamned war down there."

"Mr. President," Clum replied, "I've already had a report from Mr. Jones, who is our agent for the Cherokee Nation, and he's recommending that the attorney general order the court at Fort Smith to dismiss the charges against Proctor and the others. He's also recommending that a new United States district court be established within the boundaries of the Indian Territory. And, uh, the United States government did promise the Cherokees in the last treaty that such a court would be established."

"I'll write a letter adding my endorsement to that recommendation," Grant said. "In the meantime you proceed with your investigation."

"I'll order Enoch Hoag, our superintendent in Lawrence, Kansas, to go directly to Tahlequah and investigate personally," Clum said.

"Do that, and impress upon him the urgency of the situation, and tell the Cherokee delegation what you're doing. Maybe that will keep them off my back for a while."

Enoch Hoag, with an assistant, A. R. Banks, traveled to Fort Smith, where he presented his credentials and the letter from Commissioner Clum directing him to conduct an investigation of the Zeke Proctor affair. He went first to the office of the district attorney.

"Mr. Huckelberry," he said, "on what grounds did you issue warrants for the arrest of all these men?"

"A deputy marshal was killed, Mr. Hoag," Huckelberry replied. "Another deputy marshal had been there, and he witnessed the fight and survived it and reported to me. He gave me the names of the men on the side of Zeke Proctor during the battle."

"And that list of names includes the judge and all members of the jury?" Hoag asked.

"It does. They were all a part of a conspiracy."

"Such a conspiracy has not been proved, Mr. Huckelberry," Hoag said, "and if it existed, it existed for the purpose of influencing a trial in the Cherokee courts, a matter outside the jurisdiction of the United States."

"But we had a warrant for the arrest of Zeke Proctor for assault with attempt to murder a white man," Huckelberry said, his face red with anger and frustration.

"My understanding is that the white man in question, a Mr. James Kesterson, had married a Cherokee woman in order to obtain Cherokee citizenship rights. Did you investigate that allegation?"

"No," Huckelberry replied. "I was not involved in the case at that point. The original charges were filed with Mr. Churchill, the U.S. commissioner."

Hoag and Banks went from Huckelberry's office to that of Churchill. There they discovered that Kesterson, accompanied by the Becks, had appeared in person, accusing Zeke Proctor of attempted murder. No, Churchill told them, no one had mentioned Kesterson's marriage to an Indian woman.

"So Deputies Peavy and Owens," Hoag said, "went with a posse to the Cherokee trial to arrest Mr. Proctor and take him out of the hands of the Cherokee authorities?"

"Not exactly," Churchill said. "The Cherokees had Proctor charged with murder. We only had him charged with attempted murder. The deputies' instructions were to watch the trial. If Proctor had been found guilty and sentenced to hang, they were to forget their warrant and let well enough alone. But if the Cherokee court found him innocent, they were to arrest him on our charges and bring him in for trial in the federal court."

"I don't understand, Mr. Churchill," Hoag said. "If they had been instructed to wait for the outcome of the trial, why was there a gunfight at all? My understanding is that the trial had only just begun."

"Yes," Churchill replied. "I believe that is correct. I can't answer your question. I was not involved beyond the filing of the original charges."

Hoag and Banks went from Fort Smith to Cincinnati, where they located Joe Peavy. They met with him in a small café and ordered coffee.

"Mr. Peavy," Hoag said, "can you describe for me the actual events leading up to the gunfight at the Whitmire School?"

"Well, yes, sir, I think I can," Peavy replied. "Me and Jake Owens was going to watch the trial to see how it come out. We had orders not to arrest Zeke Proctor until after the trial, and then only if he had been found not guilty. Old White Sut Beck and a bunch of his boys was going along with us because of their interest in the case."

"Wait a minute," Hoag interrupted. "They were not a posse?"

"Well, no, they wasn't. I guess folks've been calling

them that lately, but they hadn't been sworn in or nothing. We were just riding along together."

"And were these men armed?" Hoag asked.

"I'd say they was pretty heavily armed," Peavy replied.

"Go on, Mr. Peavy," Hoag said.

"Well, we rode up to the schoolhouse, and the trial had done started. Beck told us that the Cherokee Nation had moved the trial because they was expecting a fight. The schoolhouse would be easier to defend, they said."

"That sounds to me like Mr. Beck was anticipating a fight," Hoag said. "Would you agree with that?"

"I reckon he was," Peavy replied. "They had revolvers and rifles and shotguns, and they said that the other side was looking for a fight. They could have stayed away. 'Course, the woman who was killed was a relative of theirs, so they did have an interest in the case."

"Yes," Hoag said. "Please continue."

"Well, I remember Jake telling Beck to take it easy. He said that Beck and the others had ought to leave their guns outside. 'Don't start nothing,' he said. But White Sut Beck didn't pay him no mind. He walked over to the schoolhouse door with his shotgun in his hand. I was still with the horses, but I seen him point that gun at the sheriff to make him step aside, and then I seen him go in. The next thing I know I heard a blast. Then the fight was on. I seen Jake drop, and I seen White Sut come out of the schoolhouse all shot up. I helped him to his horse and got him out of there. That's about all I can tell you."

When Peavy had left, Hoag and Banks each ordered

another cup of coffee. Banks, who had said nothing, but who had been taking notes during all the interviews, closed his notebook and looked up at Hoag.

"Where do we go from here, Mr. Hoag?" he asked.

"We're going to Tahlequah to talk with Chief Downing," Hoag replied. "What I'd really like to do is find someone who was there, who witnessed the actual killings and whose name is not on that warrant."

"Mr. Hoag?" Banks said.

"Yes?"

"How about the Whitmires?"

"Yes, sir," Eli Whitmire said. "I seen the whole thing. I was right over there looking through the window. Mama wouldn't let me go inside. She said it was crowded enough already, but I watched through the window."

They were standing in front of the Whitmire house, and Eli had pointed across the road toward the school.

"Can we take a walk over there?" Hoag asked.

"Sure," Mrs. Whitmire said. "Go ahead. When you get through, I'll have the coffee ready here. Come on back over and set a spell before you take off again."

"Thank you, ma'am," Hoag replied. "We will." He turned toward Eli again. "Come on. Let's take a look over there."

At the schoolhouse, Hoag had Banks go inside the door and wait. Then he and Eli walked around the side to look through the window. He could see Banks clearly.

"Like this?" he said.

"Yes, sir," Eli said.

"So what happened? What did you see?"

166

"Well, I seen Mr. Beck step inside, and he was holding up a shotgun."

"Did anyone inside have a gun?" Hoag asked.

"No, sir. They were just sitting there, and one of the men up there at the table was talking, and all the others was just listening to him, I guess. They didn't have guns out.

"Well, there was a deputy standing at the back of the room. He was leaning on the wall, and he was wearing guns. I guess some of the other men was wearing guns too."

"But no one had a gun in his hand?"

"Oh, no. They was sitting and listening, except the one man was talking, and the deputy, he was standing up, leaning against the wall."

"Okay, Eli. Go on. What happened next?"

"Johnson Proctor was standing inside the door right over there," Eli said, pointing through the window. "I didn't know his name then, but they told me who he was later on. Anyhow, when Mr. Beck came through the door with that shotgun, a man sitting over there stood up and pointed at him, and he hollered out something like, 'Look out. They've come to get Zeke Proctor.' Then Johnson Proctor, he stepped over in front of Mr. Beck and grabbed the gun barrel, and Mr. Beck killed him."

"Did Mr. Proctor have a gun?"

"No, sir, he didn't."

"And Mr. Beck shot him? For no reason?"

"Well, I guess maybe he didn't like Mr. Proctor grabbing his gun."

"Yeah," Hoag said. "Maybe he didn't."

—— 19 ——

Sheriff Jack Wright rode down into the pass that would lead him to the Keetoowah camp. He had been told that he would find Zeke Proctor there, and he had been asked by Chief Lewis Downing to personally meet with Zeke. Wright was not at all sure that the Keetoowahs would all know him for who he was, and even some who would recognize him might not necessarily trust him. He moved into the pass with some trepidation.

Wright had taken off his handguns and put them inside his saddlebags. His Winchester was in its scabbard. He did not want to venture out so far from home unarmed, but at the same time, he did not want to appear to the Keetoowahs like someone who had come prepared for a fight. He was not wearing his badge either. He hoped that whoever was guarding the pass would not shoot first and ask questions later, and he fervently wished that he had been fluent in the Cherokee language.

Wright was about halfway through the pass when he received his first warning.

"Go back," came the call. It had an eerie quality to it. It seemed to come from nowhere in particular. It seemed to be out there in the air. Wright looked all around, but he could see no one. He stopped riding and held his hands up over his head.

"Go back," came the voice again.

"I need to see Zeke Proctor," Wright yelled out. He felt foolish. He did not know to whom he was speaking, did not know even in which direction to shout his response. "I'm not a federal lawman."

"Go back."

"Listen to me," Wright shouted, and it occurred to him that the ones who could hear him might not even understand English. "Go back" was a common warning. Anyone could learn to shout those two words. "Listen to me. I'm Jack Wright. I come from Chief Downing with word for Zeke Proctor."

There was a long pause. Then another shout came out of the sky.

"Wait there," it said.

Wright sat still. He lowered his arms. It might be a long wait, he knew, so he might as well try to relax. He estimated that he had been there for about a half an hour when he finally saw the rider coming toward him from the direction of the valley. He squinted his eyes against the heat in the air, and then he recognized Tom Walkingstick. Still he waited. Walkingstick rode up close enough for conversation.

"'*Siyo,* Jack," he said. "We weren't sure it would really be you."

"It's me," Wright replied, "and I'm glad to see you. You know I'm not here to try to take anybody in."

"I know you'd be crazy to try it," Walkingstick said.

"That's for sure," Wright said. "Even the United States court was trying to get the army in here."

"We'll fight them if they come."

"I know you would, you crazy bastard, but they ain't coming. Can I go on in and talk to Zeke?"

"Sure," Walkingstick said. "Come on."

He turned his horse around and led the way back down the pass and into the valley. Wright had heard rumors about the camp, but the actual sight of it sent a chill down his spine. He hadn't seen anything like it since the war. There were at least fifty men, and all he could see were heavily armed. A troop of U.S. cavalry might have taken them, but it would not have been an easy job. They would have known they'd been in a fight.

He stopped his horse and dismounted when Walkingstick did, and he followed Walkingstick into the heart of the camp. Zeke Proctor was there waiting for him. As Wright neared Zeke, Zeke put out his right hand. The sheriff took it.

"Hello, Zeke," he said.

"*'Siyo.* They said you came from the chief."

"That's right. Can we sit down and talk?"

Zeke gestured toward a split log bench, and they sat down on it, side by side.

"Somebody bring Jack some coffee," Zeke said. "He's had a long ride."

"Zeke," Wright said, "I don't know how much news has reached you down here, but President Grant heard about our troubles and has ordered an investigation."

"Grant heard about me, huh?" Zeke replied. "I guess I've caused a heap of trouble."

"Quite a bit," Wright said. "He sent some men down here from the Indian Service: Mr. Hoag from Lawrence, Kansas, and another man with him. They finished their report and sent it in, and it agreed with what Mr. Jones had said, Mr. Jones, our agent."

"What had Mr. Jones said?" Zeke asked.

"Mr. Jones said that the United States didn't have any business messing in our Cherokee trial, and that White Sut Beck was responsible for starting the gunfight that resulted in the death of Deputy Owens."

Zeke looked puzzled for a moment. "They said it was Beck's fault?" he said.

"Yes. The report went to the president, and the president gave orders to the United States attorney general in Washington. The attorney general then sent out the orders to Fort Smith. The orders were that the court drop all charges against you and the others, on condition that the Cherokee Nation drop its charges against White Sut Beck."

Zeke stood up and walked a few steps away. He stood for a moment in silence, his back to Wright. At last he turned around again. "White Sut killed my brother," he said.

"Yes," Wright replied, "and you killed Polly. The concern of the United States and of the Cherokee Nation at this point is that it end here and now, that no one else get killed because of this feud, and that the Cherokee Nation not wind up in a war against the United States. The council met on this, Zeke, and they agreed."

"They're dropping the charges against White Sut?"

"That's right. They've already done it, and the charges against you have been dropped over at Fort Smith. It's like none of it ever happened."

"It happened, Jack," Zeke said. "It sure enough happened." He heaved a heavy sigh. "But if the council's voted, then I guess I'll go along. Has anyone talked to White Sut Beck?"

"I went to see him before I came to you," Wright said. "He grumbled, like you're doing. But he agreed. He said it's up to you. If you agree, then it's all over. It's been a year and a half, Zeke. It's time to end it."

Zeke twisted his wrists to grip the reversed handles of his Colts. He jerked them out and held them out in front of him, feeling their balance, studying them, thinking about the death they had dealt, the death they could still deal. He shifted them around in his hands and dropped them back into their holsters. Then he walked over close to Jack Wright.

"Well, Jack," he said, "I figured if me and White Sut Beck ever seen each other again, right after that, one of us would be dead. But now, I guess it's all over."

"It's all for the best, Zeke. Now everyone can go home."

March 1874

Zeke Proctor sat at home at the table with his sister Elizabeth and the seven children, his five and her two. They had finished eating their noon meal, and Elizabeth was starting to clear the table.

"You kids run on outside and play," she said.

They didn't have to be told twice. All of them would rather be outside than inside anytime. They ran out, leaving the door standing open behind them.

"Shut the door," Elizabeth called out, and the last

one in line turned around to shut it. "More coffee, Zeke?" Elizabeth asked.

"Yeah. Thanks."

She poured his cup full again and went on with her work.

"I heard there was a fight over at Cincinnati," she said. "You hear about it?"

"I heard," Zeke said.

"Becks and Proctors. I thought it was all supposed to be over with."

"Well," Zeke said, "it's over with, all right, but I can't keep others from fighting if they want to. And neither can old White Sut Beck. Me and him both promised that we wouldn't fight, and we've kept our word. That's all we can do."

"Are you sure about that, Zeke?" she asked. "Are you sure that's all you can do?"

Zeke didn't answer her last question. He sipped at the hot coffee and thought about the events of the last several months. After the United States government had dropped the charges against him and what it had called his gang, and the Cherokee Nation had dropped its charges against White Sut Beck, rumors had grown and spread. It was said that a general amnesty had been ordered by President Grant. Well, Zeke thought, perhaps the result was the same, but that was not exactly how it had been achieved. It had been achieved through the courts.

But that had not been the wildest rumor. People were saying that Zeke had signed a peace treaty with the United States.

"The only individual the United States ever signed a treaty with," they said.

The stories all managed to get back to him somehow. He heard them all. He also heard the stories of how he wandered the streets of Shilo and Cincinnati drunk and disorderly, firing off his weapons and frightening children. And he heard tales about how many men he had killed while he was a fugitive from the justice of the United States.

Some said that he was a bad outlaw and that the United States had finally given up on trying to capture him. Others, Cherokees, said he was a *tsgili,* a witch who could transform himself into an owl, and that, they said, was how he had managed to avoid arrest for all that time.

He finished his coffee and stood up. He took his gun belt down from a peg on the wall and strapped it around his waist. Then he put on his jacket and hat and headed for the door.

"Where you going, Zeke?" Elizabeth asked.

"I'm going out to see if I can put an end to all this," he said. "Ain't that what you said? See you after a while."

He found Jack Wright at home, and they walked out behind the sheriff's house and sat under an oak tree to smoke and talk together.

"Jack," Zeke said, "you can go see White Sut, can't you? Them Becks won't shoot at you if you go their house?"

"I can go there," said Wright. "Is there some reason I should?"

"People are telling all kinds of tales on me. On him too, I guess. The main thing is that no one seems to believe the feud is over. They say we got amnesty. They say I got a pardon. Some say I signed a treaty.

Just 20 lbs... and it's all muscle!

NOW AT LOW FACTORY-DIRECT PRICES!

YOU CAN TRY OUT THE MANTIS TILLER/CULTIVATOR IN YOUR OWN GARDEN WITH NO RISK! SEND THIS CARD TO FIND OUT HOW EASY IT IS!

Here's 20 lbs. of muscle, to blast through tough sod, till down to 10" deep and churn your your soil to a fine consistency. Our 2-cycle engine is peppy and powerful, yet gentle enough to weed and cultivate the top 3" of your garden. Thousands of these marvelous tillers have sunk their teeth into American soil for over 25 years.

Send card today!

☑ **YES!** Please rush me a **FREE VIDEO** and information on the Mantis Tiller/Cultivator and your **ONE YEAR NO-RISK TRIAL.** Tell me how I can get a **FREE BORDER EDGER** with my new tiller.

Name _____

Address _____

City _____ State _____ Zip _____

Phone _____ E-mail _____ **DEPT MT8905**

Mantis

©2006 Mantis Div. of Schiller-Pfeiffer, Inc.

Trusted Products for Mailorder Gardeners

The Best Buy Seal is a registered trademark of Consumers Digest Comm, LLC used under license

You don't have to struggle
with a big tiller to grow
a great garden!
1-800-366-6268

BUSINESS REPLY MAIL

FIRST-CLASS MAIL   PERMIT NO. 51   SOUTHAMPTON PA

POSTAGE WILL BE PAID BY ADDRESSEE

Mantis
1028 STREET RD
SOUTHAMPTON PA 18966-9941

But people are still out there fighting the Beck-Proctor fight. One of these days, someone else might even get killed."

"What do you want me to see White Sut about?" Wright asked.

"Tell him there's only one way to stop all this," Zeke replied. "Tell him that we have to show everyone. Me and him. We have to settle it in public in front of as many people as we can. Tell him I'll be in Tahlequah in four days from now. In front of the capitol. In the middle of the street. Right there. Tell him I'll be there before noontime."

"Zeke," Wright said, a little hesitant, "how do you propose to settle it? You and Sut. How?"

"Right there in the middle of the street," Zeke said, "in broad daylight in front of the capitol, I'll meet him there, and I'll shake his hand. Then it will be over with. That's how we'll do it."

"Zeke," Wright said, "I'll go right over to see him, but he's hard, and he's stubborn, and I don't know if he'll agree to it."

"He will," Zeke said. "He'll be there, and I'll be there too, and that'll be the end of it. You go tell him that. Tell him I said it."

"I'll tell him, Zeke," Wright replied. "And I'll make him listen. If you're willing, then he ought to be willing."

Zeke got up and shook Wright's hand. "I'm going home now," he said.

Wright walked with him back to where he had left his horses, and then he stood on his porch and watched Zeke riding away, leading the riderless gray. He stroked his cheek and wrinkled his brow. The man was a puzzle to him. He was a stubborn man and dangerous, but he was also honest and trustworthy, and no one, not even White Sut Beck, had ever doubted his bravery. Finally he settled the matter in his own mind. He may not understand Zeke Proctor, he told himself, but whatever the case, Zeke was one hell of a man.

Afterword

Zeke Proctor and White Sut Beck never did become friends, but after their meeting in Tahlequah, there was no more trouble between the Becks and the Proctors. The jurisdictional problems between the Cherokee Nation and the United States, so dramatically illustrated by the Zeke Proctor case, have never really been resolved. They had only been brushed aside for a time by the settlement agreed upon by both parties in 1873.

The United States district court in Indian Territory, promised by treaty and urged by President Grant, was not established until 1889. Shilo, Arkansas, became Siloam Springs, and Cincinnati languished. James Kesterson was not heard of in those parts again.

Zeke Proctor continued to operate his three farms successfully, and he as successfully raised and raced fine horses. In 1876 he was married again, this time to Margaret Downing Denton, giving him, once again, two wives at the same time. He already had ten children to raise. He would raise more, including some orphans he would take in.

During these years the legend of Zeke Proctor began to develop, for the rumors and the tall tales had not stopped with the end of the feud.

In 1876 Zeke was elected to the Cherokee senate from Goingsnake District, and in 1891 the man who had been a fugitive so much wanted by the United States District Court for Western Arkansas, received an appointment as a deputy United States marshal.

Zeke Proctor died in 1907, the year Oklahoma Territory and Indian Territory were combined to create the state of Oklahoma. That was also the year the United States government all but abolished the Cherokee Nation. It continued only through the medium of presidentially appointed principal chiefs until 1973, when the Cherokees were once again given free elections. Today the Cherokee Nation is thriving under the leadership of Principal Chief Wilma P. Mankiller.

Zeke Proctor died peacefully in his own bed. It is said that as he lay dying, the Wickliff brothers, Keetoowahs, Cherokee fugitives from United States justice, were hiding in his barn, and his last words to those gathered around him were, "Feed the boys good." He was seventy-six years old.

And the legend continued to grow.

Author's Note

The writer of historical fiction must always, I think, take some liberties with recorded facts. In dealing with the story of Zeke Proctor, I have tried to follow the events as recorded by historians, but I have also made use of some tales from a continuing oral tradition. Of course, I have imagined dialogue, motivation, thought, and specific action for the characters in my story, but I have tried to do so within the bounds of reason, based on the information available to me.

While I am in this confessional mode, I should mention that the meeting in Tahlequah between White Sut Beck and Zeke Proctor with which I have opened my novel seems not to have actually taken place until 1887, some fifteen years after the major incidents in the story. Some writers have dated it much later. Of course, it may not have taken place at all. Some few concessions must be made in the interests of art.

I want to express my thanks to Bruce Ross, to Mike

AUTHOR'S NOTE

Hadley, to Dr. Brad Agnew, to Vernon Holland, to Col. Martin Hagerstrand, to Chad Smith, to all the writers listed below, and, as always, to my wife Evelyn, for their help in the development of this book.

Finally, for readers who might be inclined to pursue the Zeke Proctor story through historical (nonfiction) sources, I recommend the following: "The Trial of Ezekiel Proctor and the Problem of Judicial Jurisdiction," by Daniel F. Littlefield, Jr., and Lonnie E. Underhill in *The Chronicles of Oklahoma,* Vol. XLVIII, Autumn 1970; "Tragedy of the Goingsnake District: The Shoot-out at Zeke Proctor's Trial," by Kelley Agnew in *The Chronicles of Oklahoma,* Vol. LXIV, 1986; "Zeke Proctor—Outlaw or Lawman?" by Olevia E. Myers in *The West,* May 1966; "The Illinois River," by T. L. Ballenger in *The Chronicles of Oklahoma,* Winter 1968–69; "Uncle Sam's Treaty With One Man," by Virgil Berry in "Notes and Documents," *The Chronicles of Oklahoma,* Vol. XXXII, Spring 1954; "One Man Peace Treaty," by Ruth Holt Payne in *Frontier Times,* August/ September 1965; *Redbird Smith and the Nighthawk Keetoowahs,* by Janey B. Hendrix, Park Hill, Oklahoma, 1983; and *The Last Cherokee Warriors,* by Phillip Steele, Gretna, Louisiana, 1987.

Tahlequah
The Cherokee Nation
June 1992

973

The *only* authorized biography of the legendary man who inspired two of the year's biggest movie events!

WYATT ☆ EARP
FRONTIER MARSHAL

"No man could have a more loyal friend than Wyatt Earp might be, nor a more dangerous enemy."
— Bat Masterson

"Earp never hunted trouble, but he was ready for any that came his way." —Jimmy Cairns, deputy marshal, Wichita, Kansas

"I am not ashamed of anything I ever did." — Wyatt Earp

POCKET
B O O K S

Available in paperback
from Pocket Books
mid-June 1994